I0542337

White Lightning Road

Harry E. Gilleland, Jr.

White Lightning Road

ISBN # 978-1-4116-8693-9

If you would like to obtain additional copies of this book, please visit www.lulu.com/harry for purchase information.

You can reach Harry E. Gilleland, Jr. by email at hgille@sport.rr.com

This book is dedicated to the late Willard and Nellie Barham of Hico, Louisiana, who raised one fine son and three wonderful daughters and who introduced me to the numerous excellent qualities of rural life. I was most fortunate to have married their daughter Linda and to have been welcomed into the warmth of their country family. It is also dedicated to Travis and Margie Hood, who introduced me to the pleasures of life along White Lightning Road.

.

About the Author

Harry E. Gilleland, Jr. is a 61-year-old southerner. Born and raised in Macon, Georgia, he earned a B.S. (1966) and a M.S. (1968) in Microbiology from the University of Georgia in Athens. Following three years of service in the U.S. Army as a captain, including a tour of duty in Vietnam, he returned to earn a Ph.D. in Microbiology from UGA in 1973. He then headed north to complete a two-year fellowship at the University of Western Ontario in London, Canada. In July of 1975 he joined the faculty of the Department of Microbiology and Immunology at Louisiana State University Health Sciences Center in Shreveport, Louisiana. After twenty-nine years of teaching microbiology to medical and graduate students and performing vaccine research, Harry retired in July of 2004. Today Harry lives in Shreveport with his wonderful wife Linda and their two dogs, Rusty and Pepper. Harry enjoys being able to engage in his passion for writing full-time.

This book is Harry's first contemporary romance story. He has previously published two books of his poetry: Poetry For The Common Man: Storoems and Poems (2003, ISBN 1411600649) and Gilleland Poetry: Storoems and Poems (2005, ISBN 1411629272). He has also penned a tale of fantasy entitled Bob the Dragon Slayer (2005, ISBN 1411633156).

Part One

~

Jenny's Story

Chapter One

As Jennifer James' car slows and turns off White Lightning Road into the driveway of her parents' house – her house now – the eyes of a remorseless killer concealed in the woods nearby watch intently. Jenny pulls under the carport and gets out. As she takes the groceries from the trunk, she stops and looks around. An uneasy feeling settles over her; somehow she senses she is being watched. She hurries inside. Once the door is closed and locked behind her, her feeling of uneasiness subsides. Maxx, her parents' Pembroke Welsh Corgi, bounds into the kitchen and jumps against her, his front feet leaning on her thighs.

"Hello, Maxx. Have you been wondering what was keeping me? I'll bet you're starved, eh, boy?"

Maxx drops his front legs to the floor and wags his tail stub in anticipation of being fed. Unlike Jenny, Maxx senses no danger outside.

Jenny opens a can of soft dog food and hardly has time to plop it into Maxx's dish before he pushes past her to gobble down the meal. Jenny walks through the dining room and down the hall to her bedroom.

As Jenny undresses to change from her business suit into shorts and t-shirt (her usual attire these days), the events of the past few hours run through her mind. She left the house in early afternoon to meet with the family's lawyer to finalize her parents' affairs. Three months earlier her parents' car was hit head-on by a pickup truck driven by a drunk driver as they topped a hill while returning from dinner in nearby Ruston. The other driver and Jenny's father were killed instantly. Jenny's mother survived in critical condition. Jenny had come from her home in Baton Rouge to bury her father and stay with her mother until she recovered...or died. She died ten days ago. Today Jenny's inheritance of their estate was completed. There was this house, 180 acres of adjoining land, a surprisingly large amount in a savings account and CD's, mineral rights that pay generous oil royalties annually, her dad's fishing boat, and her mother's car. Her parents had lived so modestly she had never realized they were so well off financially. Moreover, the lawyer assured her there would be a substantial insurance settlement to be made with the other driver's insurance company. As their only child, this inheritance would make Jenny financially secure for the first time in her life. She could take her time in deciding what to do next.

Jenny was born in New Orleans and lived there until she was fifteen years old. Then her family moved here to Lincoln Parish in north central Louisiana so that her father could accept a position with a business in Ruston, a town of about 20,000. Jenny had hated the move away from New Orleans and from all her high school friends to come to this rural environment. To make things worse, her parents bought this house out in the woods away from everything, about fifteen miles outside Ruston. The nearest neighbor was one-half mile away. The nearest store was the small gas station / grocery store / bait shop at the highway crossroads a mile away. Jenny had hated the three years she spent living here; she had counted the days until she could escape back to south Louisiana by moving to Baton Rouge to enroll in LSU. Once there, she returned to her parents' house only for Christmas and a one-week summer visit each year.

Jenny shares the belief held by many residents of Louisiana that everything important resides in the southern half of the state, with anything north of Alexandria being like another state. And there is a legitimate basis for such feelings. South Louisiana is Catholic, Cajun, fun-loving, typified by New Orleans' "Big Easy" partying lifestyle of Mardi Gras, gumbo and jambalaya, heavy drinking, the French Quarter and tailgating at LSU football games, and the attitude of "Let the good times roll!" The vast majority of Louisianians reside in the southern portion of the state. The state capital is there also in Baton Rouge. In contrast, what does northern Louisiana have? It's a land of Protestants, straight-laced values, East Texas habits and cuisine. People there have to take a trip to New Orleans to unwind! Jenny is certain she will be headed back south as soon as matters here...and her life...become more settled.

Chapter Two

Jenny awakens the next morning, determined to make some decisions about her future. The past year has been one of turmoil for her. She had reached a good place in her life prior to a year ago. She had loved attending LSU; she was a sorority girl who enjoyed the LSU experience to its maximum. She accomplished two things while at LSU. She managed to graduate with a 'C' average in a General Studies major, and she met and married Randoll James. Randy was suitably named, and their marriage had been satisfying for both. To help make financial ends meet, Randy joined the Army Reserves to supplement his entry-level salary at Hibernia Bank in Baton Rouge. Jenny took a job as an Administrative Assistant with the Department of Microbiology at LSU. For three years they were happy together, and things were proceeding according to their plans...until Randy's Army Reserve unit was mobilized and deployed to Iraq fifteen months ago. He had been on the ground as a soldier in Iraq for three months when his Humvee was blown up by a roadside bomb. His helmet and flack jacket protected his head and torso, but the blast blew away both of his legs and his right arm. He was alive when they helicoptered him to the closest Army hospital, but he died in the operating room. The news of his death devastated Jenny; images of her husband's mangled body with its missing legs and arm haunted her dreams. After months of grieving, she had just gotten her balance restored when the accident killed her father and critically injured her mother, prompting Jenny to take a leave of absence from her job and move temporarily into her parents' house. Now she finds herself, at age twenty-seven, all alone in the world, living in a place she has always hated, and burdened with painful memories associated with the place she has always loved.

Maxx jumps up onto the bed and begins licking Jenny's face as if to say "Time to get up!"

"Morning, Maxx. You must be ready to be let outside and fed breakfast, eh?" Jenny had never been a dog-person, but in the past few months she's grown extremely fond of Maxx, and now he represents a tie to her parents. They had loved him so.

Jenny lets Maxx out and opens a can of dog food for him, then gets herself a strawberry Pop Tart out of the pantry. After pouring herself a glass of milk, she sits down at the kitchen table and stares outside. *"The lawn needs mowing again,"* she thinks. It's August, and northern Louisiana has been in a drought all summer, with no rain and daily high temperatures hitting nearly 100 degrees in the shade. The ground in open areas unprotected by the shade of the trees is parched and cracked open with fissures snaking through dying grass.

"We had better get some rain soon or that lawn will be completely brown. This heat is unbearable. Down south we never have to put up with these conditions. Who would choose to live here?"

Had Jenny ever taken time to really see what her parents saw in this place they bought she would have seen 180 acres of inviting piney woods covering a valley and the slopes of two small hills enclosing it. North central Louisiana is hilly land, heavily wooded and rich with wildlife. Opossums, raccoons, and other small creatures frequently visit the yard around the house. Deer often come up to the house to eat her mother's day lilies and her father's vegetable garden, which had been a constant annoyance to her parents when they were alive. Life in rural northern Louisiana actually has much to offer for anyone receptive to its charms. Although Jenny had never been open to life in northern Louisiana, her parents had embraced the cultural differences between their previous lifestyle in New Orleans and that of rural northern Louisiana. They had come to appreciate small-community friendliness where everyone knew -- and frequently was related to by blood or marriage -- their neighbors and were always willing to be of help in any time of need. Jenny loved the sophistication of New Orleans with its concrete arteries of expressways, its historic French Quarter, its gourmet restaurants with spicy Cajun seafood dishes, its professional sports teams, its privacy where everyone was a stranger in passing, and where what you did on a daily basis could remain largely unknown to friends and neighbors. Here, big-city life was replaced by narrow, two-lane country roads winding through woody hills, by small churches attended twice on Sunday and on Wednesday evening, by small cafes serving chicken fried steak, mashed potatoes, purple hull peas, and turnip greens as their specialty, and by a complete loss of privacy. In an environment where everyone knows and recognizes everyone else, every action is noted and is a subject for the gossip that speeds its way through circles of women via telephone and circles of men as they meet at the feed or sporting goods store. The FBI would be proud to have as efficient an information-gathering network as that found in the rural communities of northern Louisiana!

No, Jenny did not consider the family's move to White Lightning Road to be a good trade. The sight of riverboats plying the Mississippi River was replaced with bass boats fishing area lakes. Trips to the Audubon Zoo were replaced by the hunting of deer with bow and arrow or high-powered rifles. Clothes shopping, once plentiful and convenient, now required a road trip to Monroe to the east or Shreveport to the west. A romantic date on Saturday night changed from dinner at an elegant French Quarter eatery, a stroll along Royal and Bourbon Streets, the sounds of jazz, and enjoying late-night chicory coffee and beignets beside the Mississippi to driving to Monroe for a movie and pizza. Jenny felt she had nothing in common with her classmates, who came from families that farmed, raised chickens by the tens of thousands in massive chicken houses, and hunted and fished as a way of life. While Jenny grew up in a world of shopping malls, city parks, and museums, these kids were active in 4-H raising chickens, calves, pigs, and sheep to win prizes at the state fair. In her eyes, the girls here were plain and unworldly, and the boys were rough and country. Jenny's three years of high school felt like a prison sentence; she could not have withstood it had it not been for Sally Benson. Sally was Jenny's only close friend. Sally's family had moved to White Lightning Road from Dallas the same year Jenny's family had moved here from New Orleans. Sally was Jenny's soul mate – two urban refugees lost in the woods. They spent the three years bemoaning their loss of big-city life and constantly plotting their escape. They were inseparable in school and out. They listened to music, looked through fashion magazines, and rode in their fathers' cars through the campus of Louisiana Tech in Ruston ogling and flirting with the college boys. They kept one another sane. They became like sisters. Then Jenny fled to Baton Rouge for college, and Sally left for Dallas to get married. Sally was the one good thing Jenny had found in north Louisiana.

A knock on the door startles Jenny out of her daydreaming. She walks to the door and looks out; standing there is Michael Garrott, her parents' nearest neighbor. He owns the property adjoining her parents' 180 acres and lives in the house one-half mile away. Michael, a man in his mid-thirties, is tall and good-looking in a tanned, outdoorsy way, with unkempt black hair and a three-day stubble on his face. He has on blue jeans and a tight t-shirt that shows his well-muscled torso to good effect. Apprehension suddenly grips Jenny; she is alone, a mile away from any help, and Michael Garrott is a man to be fearful of. His wife and young daughter were killed four years ago in an automobile crash; a man crossed over the centerline with his car and sideswiped their vehicle, sending it tumbling down the embankment and into a tree. The driver tested positive for drugs and pled guilty to two counts of vehicular manslaughter. He was a member of a prominent family in Ruston and served only one year in jail, with the remainder of his sentence reduced to probation. Michael was quite vocal about how unfair it was that the man got off with only one year in jail for killing his wife and daughter. The week after the man was released from jail, his body turned up on the main street of Ruston late one night with three bullet holes to the heart. Even though Michael proclaimed his innocence, everyone "knew" Michael killed the man for revenge. There was simply no evidence to prove he was in fact the killer. Now Michael Garrott is considered to be a man not to be crossed under any circumstances. From that killing on, most people began to avoid Michael whenever possible, and he became rather unfriendly toward all. And now, here he is, standing outside Jenny's kitchen door.

Chapter Three

Jenny opens the door just a crack and asks, "Hi, what can I do for you?" The tension in her voice reveals her apprehension.

"I've come to buy your parents' land," Michael declares in a hard, all-business voice.

"It's not for sale at present. I haven't decided yet what I intend to do with the property." Jenny isn't sure she wants to let a suspected murderer own her parents' home.

"That won't do! I've got plans for this land. Your father promised me I could buy it if he ever decided to sell it. I'm here to buy this place," Michael says, with his voice sounding even sterner than before. Then he adds, "I know you don't plan to live here."

"I said it's not for sale. I'll let you know if anything changes," Jenny replies firmly as she closes the door. She watches Michael turn away and head across the yard. She notices he has no car, just as he disappears into the woods, heading back toward his house. *"The nerve of the man!"* she thinks, *"He acts like he already owns this place!"* Anger wells up inside her as she considers how casually this man just trespassed on her parents' land.

The next day Jenny makes a bread and milk run to the gas station / grocery store / bait shop down at the crossroads. As she places her few items on the counter, the storeowner, Bubba Wadsom, greets her with a cheery "Good mornin'. Gonna be another scorcher today."

"Seems every summer day is a scorcher up here," Jenny tosses back in reply.

Bubba Wadsom is a large man, somewhat overweight as well as having a large frame. He has owned this store for forty years, and he knows everyone living on White Lightning Road...and everything about them all. More gossip than gasoline passes through his store. "I hear Michael Garrott is finally gonna get his hands on your parents' place. He's had his eye on that land for years."

Surprised by his comment, Jenny answers, "My land is not for sale. When it is, I may, or may not, sell to Mr. Garrott."

"Well, honey, I'm sure you know you don't want Garrott mad at you. It ain't healthy. Everybody knows he's determined to have that place," Bubba says, sounding fatherly, as if to warn her.

Fed up with this line of conversation, Jenny demands, "How much do I owe you?"

She pays and heads for the door. Bubba calls after her, "Sorry 'bout your mama. It was a fine funeral tho'."

As soon as she opens her front door, Maxx bolts by her, running toward the woods. He stops abruptly, barking ferociously as he begins to back away toward the house. "What's out there, Maxx? You got some varmint spotted?" Jenny calls out as she cautiously walks over to stand beside Maxx, peering intently into the woods to see if she can discern the object of Maxx's attention. After seeing nothing, she tells Maxx, "Whatever it was, it must be gone now. Good boy, Maxx. You do a great job keeping the varmints away." She reaches down and gives Maxx a pat on the head, to which he responds by forgetting the woods and turning to jump up with his legs against her thighs, begging for more attention. As they walk back inside, Jenny thinks, *"I'm sure glad I have Maxx to alert me to anything that comes into the yard."*

That afternoon the telephone rings; Jenny is surprised. At the time of her arrival for her father's funeral, a constant stream of telephone calls and food deliveries to the house had begun. It had continued all during her mother's stay in the hospital, with friends and neighbors calling daily to check on her mother's condition or to drop off some home-cooked casserole or baked goods "since Jenny needs to eat right and hasn't time to cook for herself". Soon the freezer began to overflow. The first few days after her mother's death, the phone rang constantly with neighbors and members of her parents' church calling to give their condolences and ask what could they bring over to help out. Jenny had told everyone she needed nothing, but that hadn't stopped the steady delivery of food for the next two days. Most of it had gone to waste. After a few more days, the calls and visits had ceased. The phone had not rung for four days. Jenny picks up the receiver on the third ring, wondering who it could possibly be.

"Hi, Jen. It's Sally. I'm so sorry about missing your mom's funeral, but I had to be in court in Dallas getting rid of husband number two. On top of that, Jody got sick with a bad cold. Things have been rather hectic lately. I've come to stay at Mother and Dad's for a few weeks. At least that was the plan. I got here yesterday, and they are already driving me crazy! How would you like some company for a day or two?"

Sally's parents' place is down White Lightning Road a few miles toward the town of Homer. Sally had escaped to Dallas at age eighteen by marrying the first man that proposed marriage. That first marriage lasted less than a year, but Sally stayed in the Dallas area. She remarried two years later and moved to Plano. She and husband number two had been married for five years and have a three-year-old son, Jody. Sally's world was shaken one afternoon several months ago. She had called Jenny, upset and wailing into the telephone, "The bastard has a mistress who came crying to me today. Seems he got her knocked up, then told her to get lost. For months, to keep her interested in the affair, he had been promising her he would leave me soon. I threw him out, Jenny. Tomorrow I am filing for divorce. She's welcome to him." Sally had now made him a man of his word.

"Sure, Sally, I'd love some company. When can you come?" Jenny answers enthusiastically.

"Look out your window. I should be pulling into your driveway in about a minute."

"Pretty sure of yourself, weren't you?" Jenny says with a smile in her voice. Having Sally stay with her for a few days is sure to lift Jenny's spirits.

Sally's car turns into the driveway, and Jenny goes outside to welcome her. Sally gets out and hugs Jenny like a long-lost sister. "Boy, it's great to see you, Jen. Being together should be good therapy for us both," Sally says, tightening her hug. "Oh, let me tend to Jody. Hope you don't mind having a three-year-old kid underfoot," Sally adds as she releases the hug. She opens the back car door and unbuckles Jody's seatbelt, sending him bounding out of the car and heading for the woods. "Jody, get back here. Right now, young man!" Sally yells. Reluctantly, Jody turns around and heads back to his mother.

"It's great to see you again, too. Jody sure is growing up fast. Looks like he's all boy! We have so much catching up to do; it'll be a late night sitting up talking tonight," Jenny says, as they all go inside the house. As Jenny is closing the door, she hesitates and looks toward the woods. She has an uneasy feeling that they are being watched. She firmly shuts the door and locks it.

Jenny notices how tired Sally's eyes appear and how she has gained weight since Jenny saw her three months ago. Sally is short at five foot three; she has long, red hair and freckles, with a small frame and small breasts. Normally trim and fit, Sally tends to gain weight during stressful periods. Obviously the divorce has taken its toll on her. Usually easy to laugh and possessing a bubbly personality, Sally seems somewhat subdued today.

That night they stay up until midnight talking and laughing about husbands, the joys of raising children, and life in the big city versus rural life. They cry over Sally's husband's adultery and her recent divorce and over the recent deaths of Jenny's father and mother. Since going their separate ways after high school, they have managed to be together for all of each other's big events – Jenny was Maid of Honor for both of Sally's weddings, and Sally was Matron of Honor for Jenny's marriage to Randy; Jenny came to visit Sally for a week at the birth of Jody; and Sally had come to support Jenny after the death of Randy and more recently the death of her father and her mother's hospitalization three months ago. In between their in-person visits, they have acted as each other's counselor and sounding board through telephone calls, sometimes talking only monthly, other times weekly, and at worst times daily. Jenny realizes as they talk tonight how lost she would be without Sally in her life. Jenny has no close relatives and practically no relatives at all. Her mother was an only child. Her father had only one sibling, an older sister who is a nun. Jenny rarely sees her, primarily at family funerals lately. Both sets of Jenny's grandparents are deceased. Sally is more than a friend; she is Jenny's substitute family now.

At midnight, Sally announces, "I'd better be heading off to bed. Whenever I make a late night of it, Jody is sure to make it an early morning. He'll be waking up around 7:30. Trust me."

Jenny gets up, and as she hugs Sally extra hard, says, "Sally, you are my rock. I don't know how I'd manage without you."

Sally answers, "I feel the same way about you, girl. You know, you should come to Plano and live with Jody and me for a while. It would do us both good. We could hunker down and lick our wounds together."

"I just might take you up on your offer. First, I have to decide whether I want to stay in Baton Rouge or not. Let's sleep on it. Sleep well," Jenny responds, liking the idea at first impression.

Chapter Four

In the morning, Jenny announces to Sally that she's made her decision. "I'm going to sell this place. I need to be in the city; small-town life is not for me. But, I'm not going back to Baton Rouge. There are just too many painful memories there. Instead, I think I'll take you up on the offer to move to Plano. You sure you want me as a roommate for awhile?"

A huge smile breaks out on Sally's face. "Great, Jen! I got the house in Plano in the divorce settlement. It's plenty big enough for the three of us. You can take as long as you want in finding your own place and a new job. It'll be wonderful therapy for us both."

They spend the rest of the day chatting like the schoolgirls they once were about their plans to live together in Plano. Excitement and laughter fill their day.

As darkness approaches, Jenny steps outside to call Maxx. She realizes she hasn't seen him around all afternoon. It's not like Maxx to wander far away from the house; he has always been an inside dog that rarely leaves the yard to enter the woods. Jenny calls and calls...but Maxx never appears. Worry replaces her mood of happiness, and she hopes Maxx will return home as soon as it gets good and dark.

Maxx is gone all night. In the morning Jenny decides to go searching for him in the woods behind the house. Sally offers to accompany her. "No, Sally, you need to stay home with Jody. I can search faster by myself without a three-year-old along."

Jenny walks deeper and deeper into the piney woods. She hasn't been in these woods for years, and she seldom ventured very far into them those years she had lived here as a teenager. Malls were more to her liking than woods. She repeatedly calls out "Maxx. Here, Maxx!" She's still hoping to see him come bounding up to her out of the woods. She has walked almost to the end of her property line when she hears rustling in the woods to her left. She freezes and listens intently. There it is again! Something is definitely moving in the thicket on her left. As she slowly walks in that direction, sweat drips from her brow. Her t-shirt is now wet and clinging to her from the heat, exertion, and nerves. Her muscles tighten as she enters the thicket. Seeing nothing, she relaxes her tense shoulders. Suddenly, in a flurry of noise and movement, three large birds appear out of the woods and rush at her. Jenny screams and runs as fast as she can toward home. *"What the hell were those? Ostriches? What in hell are ostriches doing roaming the woods of Louisiana?"* races through her mind as she runs. As she nears the house, she trips and tumbles down. She gets up, knees bleeding and legs and arms scratched, and resumes running to the house.

She bursts inside the house, scaring Jody and causing him to start crying. Sally comes rushing into the kitchen. Shock and concern show on her face as she sees Jenny standing before her panting, dirty, and bloodied. "What happened to you?"

"Ostriches! I was attacked by a flock of ostriches in the woods behind the house. How long have there been ostriches roaming the woods? We need to call someone and warn the public!" Jenny manages to stammer out amidst her panting.

Sally breaks out laughing. "You probably scared the poor things as much as they scared you. They're probably still running away. Besides, they aren't ostriches at all. They're emus. Dad told me that several people around here tried emu ranching back when it was a popular get-rich-quick scheme a few years ago. When their business went bust, some ranchers just let their emus loose rather than kill them. Quite a few hunters have been startled by crossing paths with an emu in the woods. Dad says old man Parker gave up turkey hunting last year when he went looking for turkeys and encountered an emu instead. Scared him half to death. Just calm down, and we'll get you cleaned up. No sign of Maxx?"

As Jenny begins to calm down, the humor in the situation becomes apparent. "Well, they should warn the public of the emu danger in the woods around here. That's all I have to say on the matter." Her smile grows larger and larger as she imagines how foolish she must have looked had anyone been watching her encounter with the emus. "We just won't tell anyone else about this, okay?"

"Did you see any sign of Maxx while you were out chasing emus?" Sally inquires again.

"No, but I'll search the woods in a pattern tomorrow, if he doesn't turn up today." Jenny's mood turns somber again at the thought of her lost dog. "Surely he'll come home today."

The next morning, Maxx is still missing.

Chapter Five

Mid-morning, Jenny sets out searching the woods. Starting where her property fronts White Lightning Road, she walks through the woods in a semi-circular arc until she comes to where it meets the road again. Then she walks twenty yards farther out and begins to follow that arc back through the woods until she gets back to the road. She is walking her fifth arc through the woods when she approaches a small hollow. She notices a swarm of flies hovering over a spot. Cautiously, she draws nearer and nearer until she can hear the flies' buzzing resonating in her head. Then, Jenny screams out, "No! No! Not Maxx!" Tears pour from her eyes and her heart leaps into her throat. She stands over Maxx's bloodied and mutilated body, which seems so small to her now. Blood has soaked into the ground, making a nightmarish splotch several feet across. Jenny turns away. She walks back toward the house, trying to remain erect as her knees grow weaker and weaker. Just as she walks onto the carport, her knees give way. She slumps against the wall, sobbing uncontrollably. Sally hears the sobs and comes out to investigate the sounds.

"Call 9-1-1. Tell them to send the sheriff out. Maxx has been murdered. That son of a bitch murdered Maxx!" Jenny's words are barely recognizable between her sobs.

"Who killed Maxx? Why would anyone want to kill Maxx? What are you talking about, Jen?" Sally asks in her confusion. She walks toward Jenny to comfort her and help her inside.

"CALL 9-1-1. That bastard Garrott wants me off this land. I'm sure he killed Maxx as a warning to me. CALL 9-1-1 NOW!" Jenny screams at her friend.

Sally hurries inside. Jenny hears her talking. "Yes, we have an emergency. Please send a sheriff's deputy to the old Sinclair place on White Lightning Road immediately. Someone has killed our dog. What? Why, yes, this is a real emergency. Jenny thinks Michael Garrott did it to intimidate her. What? Okay, just get someone here as soon as you can."

Sally comes back outside. "Let's get you on your feet and inside so you can lie down and compose yourself before the deputy arrives. They didn't seem to think a dead dog was an emergency, but they agreed to send a deputy as soon as one's available."

Sally helps Jenny inside and, to calm her while they wait on the deputy to arrive, she makes Jenny drink some water, then leads her to the sofa. They sit together with Sally's arms around Jenny as Jenny babbles on about Garrott being a known killer who is demanding she sell her land to him. Who else would kill Maxx? Finally, Jenny cries out her anger, and Sally convinces her to lie down on the sofa for a while, "just until the sheriff comes."

Nearly two hours pass before they finally hear a car pulling into the driveway. Jenny walks to the door and sees a deputy get out of the patrol car. The man is about her age. He's handsome, with thick, blond hair cut militarily short, and an athletic body. He seems vaguely familiar.

"How do you do, ma'am? What's this about a dead dog?" the deputy asks.

"I found Maxx, my Corgi, butchered in the woods. Michael Garrott wants me off this land. I just know he killed Maxx as a warning to me. Everyone around here seems to know he's a murderer. Two days after I tell him I'm not sure I'll sell my land to him, my dog goes missing. Are you telling me that is just coincidence?" Jenny blurts out, her lower lip trembling and tears welling up in her eyes as she fights to maintain her composure.

"Ma'am, dogs go missing or turn up dead around these parts all the time. Usually it's a pack of coyotes that takes them. No reason to think Mr. Garrott had anything to do with this, now is there?" the deputy replies dismissively. Jenny immediately senses he does *not* intend to pursue her complaint.

"Can you at least examine the scene of the murder and gather any evidence you might find? Maybe you can prove he did this," Jenny pleads.

"No problem, ma'am; lead the way," the deputy answers. He then follows her into the woods.

As they walk, Jenny says, "You think this is a waste of your time, don't you? I guess a dead dog is not high on your list of crimes. Is that why it took you two hours to respond?" Her frustration with the deputy's attitude shows through.

"Ma'am, we were working a big pile-up with injuries up on I-20. That was just a bit more important than your dead dog, don't you agree?" the deputy answers curtly, as his shoulders straighten and his face turns red with aggravation at her remark.

"Yes, okay, I guess. But, this is serious to me. I feel threatened by Garrott. Everyone knows he wants me off this land. And you know his reputation as a killer," Jenny answers, refusing to back down.

After they walk farther into the woods, the deputy says, "You're the Jenny Sinclair that went to high school here, aren't you? Do you remember me?"

"Yes, I'm Jenny Sinclair, but my married name now is James. You *do* look familiar; who are you?" Jenny tries to get a look at his nametag on his shirt pocket.

"I'm Bobby Yale. I was on the football team in high school. I asked you out on a date once, remember? You told me to shove off because you would never date a dumb jock like me," the deputy replies coldly.

Embarrassment causes Jenny's face to flush. Fortunately, they arrive at the site where she found Maxx's body, and the subject changes. The deputy briefly studies the scene, poking at Maxx's remains and

25

examining the ground around the site. Then he says, "Looks like some animal predator did this. The ground is too hard from the drought to see any tracks or footprints, but it looks like something devoured almost all of his body except the hide, feet and head. No evidence here to suspect Mr. Garrott had anything to do with this. We country folks realize that dogs get themselves killed by coyotes or dog packs all the time. No need to make anything more of this. Certainly no reason to go bothering Mr. Garrott with this."

They walk in silence back to the house. The deputy gets into his patrol car and drives away. Jenny thinks she sees a smirk on his face as he glances back at her. *"Damn! Too bad I didn't go on that date with him back in high school. Maybe he would have been more cooperative just now."*

Sally comes outside and asks, "Well, are they going to investigate Garrott about this?"

"No. The deputy treated it almost as a joke. We're going to have to deal with this on our own." Jenny turns and marches inside the house.

Chapter Six

Jenny spends a restless night grieving over losing all her immediate family members within the past year – first her husband, then her father, finally her mother – and now even the family pet, poor old Maxx. *"Thank God, Mom and Dad weren't alive to see the mutilated body of their beloved Corgi. The shock would have killed them,"* she thinks sometimes around 3 a.m. Toward dawn her grief has turned to blind fury at Michael Garrott. He won't be allowed get away with murder this time, not if she has anything to say about it! Finally, close to dawn, Jenny falls into a fitful sleep.

Jenny awakens at 8 a.m. to hear Sally speaking loudly with someone at the kitchen door. Jenny strains to catch what she is saying. "No, you can't speak to her. You've got *some* nerve showing up here after what you did. She's asleep. Go away before I call the sheriff on you!"

Jenny gets out of bed, momentarily looks around for Maxx until yesterday's events spring to mind, and then pulls on a robe, while heading down the hall. She arrives at the kitchen door to see Michael Garrott standing there, looking upset. He sees Jenny and demands, "Let me talk to you. We need to clear something up. Talk to me!"

"Let him in, Sally. I want to tell the son of a bitch a thing or two myself," Jenny responds, her fury returning.

Michael steps inside the kitchen, then begins, "You owe me an apology, Jenny James. I was at the crossroads store this morning, and Bubba told me it's all over Lincoln Parish that you're claiming I killed your dog yesterday. Why would you ever think I would kill your parents' dog? I have enough trouble with people gossiping about me without you stirring up resentment toward me, too. You even tried to sic the law on me, I hear."

As he speaks, his tone softens from anger to hurt. Jenny is surprised to see that he seems genuinely offended that he has been accused of being a dog killer. She offers, "But you were so awful to me when you were here before. You almost demanded that I get off my own property and sell it to you. Why would someone with your past history hesitate to kill a mere dog if it gets you something you want badly?"

"What do you know of my past history? Do you believe all the unfounded gossip you hear about someone you don't know? My wife and child were killed by a doped-up man who got off nearly scot-free because his family is important in this parish. The whole parish stood idly by and allowed him to walk out of jail free. I didn't kill him, but I'm sure glad someone else did. I denied having anything to do with his murder at every opportunity, but no one believed me. So, I quit denying it. Let the people around here think whatever they choose about me. I wanted nothing more to do with them anyway. Thinking I am a murderer keeps them out of my business. But I would never kill anyone's pet dog. Never!" Michael speaks with such sincerity that Jenny begins to waver in the hatred that she has worked up for him.

"You don't care if people think you murdered a man, but you don't want them to think you would kill a dog?"

"Damn right…if the man is scum like that man was. A dog is worth more than he was, and a dog deserves better treatment," Michael replies earnestly.

"Well, maybe I was hasty to accuse you. It just seemed like something a murderer wouldn't hesitate to do. I know you want me off this land," Jenny says defensively, her voice revealing her growing doubt.

"Yes, I want this land. Your father promised it to me should they ever move. He told me you would not live here for anything in this world. It adjoins mine, and I have plans for this property. But, I would never have hurt Maxx. Please, you must believe me about this." His demeanor has softened completely from its initial angry hostility to one of seeking acceptance and understanding.

In response, Jenny softens as well. "All right, I won't tell anyone else that I think you killed Maxx to intimidate me. If you're innocent, I'm sorry to have offended you." In spite of her suspicions, Jenny finds herself wavering in her confidence that this man was capable of killing Maxx.

"Then I'll take my leave." With that, Michael strides to his car and drives away without looking back.

Sally speaks first. "He was slick, eh? Damned convincing! I meet lots of men like that in Dallas. They can talk you into anything – into a lemon of a used car, out of your panties, or to trust them when you know better."

Jenny is quiet at first; then she says, "I don't know, Sally, but I think he was telling the truth."

To this, Sally rolls her eyes and says, "Girl, let me interest you in some swamp land down on the coast!" She laughs out loud. "It's prime real estate and would make you a *great* investment. It's only under water at high tide."

"I may be being gullible, but I think I can trust him."

Chapter Seven

Several days pass uneventfully. Sally and Jenny spend the time sorting through Jenny's parents' possessions, deciding what to keep, what to give to charity, and what to trash. Many items bring back a flood of memories, accompanied by a flood of tears. It's amazing what parents save from their child's youth. Jenny uncovers grade school pictures she drew, old report cards, and other mementos spanning her entire lifetime. What does one do with such treasures hoarded for so many years by one's mother? And what of the collections her parents had so lovingly assembled during their lives? Her mother had amassed a collection of dozens of salters with tiny sterling silver spoons. Each spoon is worth at least ten dollars, and the salters more than that. How does a daughter dispose of her mother's prized collection? Her father had collected old bottles by the hundreds. What is she to do with a bunch of old bottles? Jenny faces decision after decision about what to do with her parents' lifetime accumulation of possessions. After three days, Sally finally says. "Why don't we take a break for a couple of days? This is hard on you. I can see it's wearing you down."

Jenny replies, with a heavy sigh, "No, we have to get through with it all. Every drawer, every closet in every room must be cleaned out before I can sell the house. The longer we take to finish this, the longer I have to stay here. I'm ready to be done with this and on my way to Dallas."

Mid-afternoon that day they are sorting through her mother's clothes closet when they hear a knock at the kitchen door. Jenny is surprised to find Michael Garrott waiting there. She has been doing a lot of thinking about him over the past three days. Now she feels sorry for him; he lost his wife and child so violently, and then the whole community labeled him a murderer. He must be a very lonely and injured man.

"I think I may have an idea what happened to your dog," he says as she opens the door.

"Please come in and tell me about it," she offers as she opens the door widely. "Would you care for some coffee, or maybe a Coke?"

Michael seems surprised at such a cordial welcome. He visibly relaxes and replies with a smile that is as engaging as any Jenny has ever seen, "Coffee would be nice. I was up early this morning."

They settle into seats at the kitchen table, staring intently at each other as if trying to figure each other out. Michael breaks the silence. "I found one of my larger calves killed this morning. It looks to me like we have a large predator in the area. I don't think this slaughter was done by coyotes or a pack of dogs."

Jenny's brow wrinkles. She asks, "What sort of 'large predator' are you suggesting?" She's thinking, *"Great! First emus running loose in the woods scaring people and now this."*

Michael hesitates before answering. "I'm thinking it may be a bear. There are some black bears in this state that can get fairly large, but it would be unusual for one to be hunting this close to humans. They usually try to avoid any contact with people. They've learned the hard way that humans are dangerous enemies. A bear that has lost his fear of humans would be a *very* dangerous animal."

Michael pauses to ponder this notion; then he continues, "Bears frequently revisit sites of a kill. I plan on leaving some poisoned bait near the slaughtered calf. Maybe I can kill him that way."

Jenny takes in what he has said. "Why don't you also put some of your bait in the woods here where Maxx was killed? I want Maxx's killer dead!"

"I could do that, if you would show me where Maxx was found. I have some of the poisoned bait in my car." Michael is eager to please her and to earn her confidence.

"Fine. Come on, and I'll take you there now," Jenny agrees.

Jenny tells Sally where she and Michael are going; then they head for the woods. As they walk, she studies him. *"He walks confidently, like a man sure of himself,"* she thinks. Michael is tall, about six foot two, with the well-muscled body of a man who either works out or works hard. He has a deep suntan, and today he is clean-shaven. Jenny decides he is quite handsome, much more so than she had realized in their previous meetings when her perceptions were clouded by fear and apprehension.

Michael also watches Jenny as they walk. She is tall at five foot eight, with a slender build and nice breasts shown off to good advantage by her snug t-shirt. Her hair is light brown and cut short. She has an attractive face, although he wouldn't call her beautiful. Today she seems much more attractive to him than she had in their previous meetings.

They arrive at the small hollow where Maxx's ravaged body lies. "I can't see Maxx again in that condition...with the blood and all. I'll wait for you here." Jenny's eyes fill with tears, and her lower lip trembles slightly.

Michael responds, "Sure. Stay back. I'll take care of this." He busies himself putting out the poisoned meat and placing Maxx's skimpy remains in the bag he'd brought the meat in. "Let's get back to the house," he suggests once he has finished.

They walk back in silence. Michael notices tears trickling down Jenny's cheeks, and he wants to comfort her. "Would you like me to bury Maxx's remains somewhere near the house? Maybe in a place that was special to your parents?"

Jenny is surprised by his kindness. "That would be awfully nice of you. How about over there under that big oak tree? Maxx used to lie there in the shade a lot."

Michael gets a shovel from the tool shed, but the ground is hard as rock due to the drought. He takes the garden hose over to the spot and soaks the ground to soften it. He quickly digs a deep hole, places the bag with Maxx's remains in it, and replaces the dirt. Then he asks Jenny, "Care to say anything over him?"

Jenny says softly, almost in a whisper, "You were a good dog, Maxx, and you were well-loved."

With that they walk back to the kitchen door. Jenny asks, "Would you like to stay for supper?"

Michael pauses; then he replies, "Thanks, but I reckon I'd better be getting back to my place. Maybe some other time."

Jenny feels disappointed as she watches him drive away.

Chapter Eight

The next morning Sally is outside with Jody when Jenny hears her call out, "Jenny, you'd better come out here and see this."

Jenny walks outside and sees Sally standing at Maxx's grave. "What's up?" Jenny asks as she draws nearer.

"See for yourself," Sally says as she points at the ground.

There in the moistened dirt around Maxx's grave is a set of large paw prints where some animal has walked around the gravesite. "Michael had better see this," Jenny says as she heads for the house.

She finds the local phonebook and looks up Michael's number; she dials it and waits for him to answer. She is about to hang up when he finally answers.

"Michael, this is Jenny James. Can you come over right away? There's something here you need to see. I think your bear was prowling around my yard last night."

"I'll be right there" is his immediate response.

In only a few minutes, Michael's car turns into Jenny's driveway. Michael gets out and walks over to the two women, who are standing at Maxx's gravesite. He asks, "Well, what have you got to show me?" Then he sees the paw prints. A look of puzzlement crosses his face. He reaches inside his pocket for his cell phone and starts dialing a number.

"Who are you calling?" Jenny asks.

"A good friend of mine. He's a game warden and the best tracker I know. He needs to see these tracks."

Before long, there are several game wardens and park rangers assembled in Jenny's yard studying the tracks and taking measurements. Sally and Jenny take Jody inside and prepare coffee for all the men. Soon, Michael comes inside and surprises them with the experts' conclusion. "Well, it may be tracks from our predator, but those aren't bear tracks."

Jenny's face tightens up with confusion. "What is it if it isn't a bear?"

"You're probably not going to believe this because we're not sure it's possible, but it appears to be the tracks of a rather large mountain lion," Michael answers. Then he adds, "There hasn't been a confirmed sighting of a mountain lion in Louisiana in decades. Every so often some driver claims to see one crossing a highway or some hunter thinks he catches a glimpse of one in the woods, but those accounts usually don't hold up. We're all a bit mystified by what you have in your yard. The game wardens are making a cast of the paw prints for the record."

Jenny thinks a minute, then asks, "Where would a mountain lion have come from, and why would it be coming so close to humans?"

"We were just discussing that. He could have migrated from some nearby home range, maybe from over in Texas. Maybe he's old and not able to hunt deer and wild game anymore. Maybe he's injured or sick. The drought has forced a lot of animals out of the woods to seek water and food near houses and barns. Maybe this lion is following his prey. We don't know how to explain it. None of us has ever heard of anything like this before," Michael explains. "Once word of this gets out, you're apt to have lots of people roaming around in your yard and woods. This is an important find."

"Are we in any danger living here? Do y'all expect him to come back? What should I do?" Images of a mountain lion lurking around outside her house in the dark of night looking for a kill play in Jenny's mind.

Michael smiles reassuringly. "That cat is probably long gone by now. Mountain lions range over an extremely large territory. You're in more danger from the curiosity-seeking people who'll be trampling over your property in the next few days."

The men finish their examination, make their casts of the paw prints, take pictures, and finally everyone, including Michael, leaves. Jenny turns to

Sally and says, "We'd better stay close to the house and keep Jody inside. How do they know that the lion has moved on?" A shiver passes down Jenny's spine as she looks out at Maxx's grave.

Within hours the news of a large cougar roaming the woods at the old Sinclair place off White Lightning Road has spread -- first by Bubba, then by radio, and finally by television. A Monroe television station has a news crew on the scene filming a report on the paw prints in Jenny's yard, newspaper reporters from both Shreveport and Monroe are calling for information, and gun-toting hunters are showing up and heading into the woods. Sally watches the activity through the kitchen window, then turns to Jenny with a look of concern. "Jen, it's getting crazy out there. You'd better call the Sheriff's Department and have them send someone over to control this crowd."

Jenny places the call to the sheriff's office, but by the time a deputy shows up the woods are full of men with rifles searching for the cougar. The deputy who arrives just happens to be Bobby Yale.

Deputy Yale steps out of his patrol car and surveys the scene. Then he reaches inside for his radio microphone and speaks into it before closing his door and walking over to the kitchen door where Jenny and Sally are waiting. He says, "Looks like you ladies have a real circus out here. I called for backup. If you will just stay in the house, I'll start getting things under control."

Just as he finishes his sentence, a shot rings out in the woods. It is followed by what sounds like a battle from a war zone. "Jesus! What are those fools shooting at," the deputy exclaims as he heads for the woods.

Jenny and Sally step outside onto the carport. Shouting is heard from the woods. "Maybe they killed the cougar," Sally says hopefully.

Soon one of the hunters runs past them toward his pickup truck. Jenny calls after him, "What's going on? Did they kill the mountain lion?"

The man stops running long enough to yell, "No, ma'am. But we shot us a couple of the biggest damned birds you ever did see."

In exasperation Jenny says to Sally, "They shot the damned emus!"

Several more sheriff cars pull into the driveway; the deputies round up the hunters and send them away. Afterwards, Deputy Yale walks over to Jenny and assures her, "Things are back to normal here. We'll keep a deputy down at the driveway for a while to turn away any would-be trespassers. Now you just let us know if you have any more problems." As he turns to walk away, he pauses, looks back, and adds, "Aren't you sorry about all those accusations you made about Michael Garrott the last time I was here?" With a smirk, he gets into his car and drives away.

Jenny isn't sure whether to get mad or to feel ashamed. Sally has no problem deciding. "What an asshole!" she hisses.

Jenny and Sally walk back inside, happy that the commotion has finally stopped.

Chapter Nine

      As they are walking inside, the telephone rings. Jenny answers it; then she hands the phone to Sally. "It's your mother."

      Jenny walks into the den, but she still can hear Sally's end of the conversation: "Yes, Mother... No, Mother...That's not true, Mother...Yes, Mother...Yes, Mother...I don't agree, Mother...Yes, Mother... All right, Mother...Yes, I said all right. I'll be there in an hour. Bye, Mother...Geeez."

      Sally hangs up the telephone and says to Jenny with a mixture of exasperation and anger in her voice, "Jen, I've got to go stay back over at Mother and Dad's. They've seen all the news about there being a mountain lion prowling your yard, and they're having a fit about their grandson being in mortal danger. She didn't mention anything about me getting eaten by a lion, just her precious grandson. I have to go back over there to stay, or I'll never hear the end of it. Sorry to leave you."

Jenny smiles. "I totally understand, Sally. And it might actually be safer for you and Jody. For this once, your mother may be right."

Sally gathers her and Jody's things and prepares to depart. Jenny walks them out to the car, then kisses Jody on the cheek and says her goodbyes to him. She hugs Sally tightly and says, "We still need to work out the details of my move to Plano. I'll call you in the next day or two. Don't let your mother drive you completely crazy in the meanwhile."

Sally replies, "Jen, maybe you should come with me to my folks' place. You might not be safe here alone. Trust me."

Jenny gives a small laugh. "YOU have to stay with your mother. I don't! Seriously, I will be perfectly fine. Besides, I can always call Michael. He is just minutes away."

As Sally climbs behind the wheel of her car, she says, "Right. Michael. Just remember what I told you about used cars, panties, and swampland. I still don't trust him, Jen." She closes the door and drives away, leaving Jenny standing alone in the yard.

The afternoon speeds by. Jenny decides to watch the evening news on one of the Monroe television channels. To her horror, they feature the story of finding paw prints of a mountain lion as their lead-in story and follow it with a major segment of the news portion of the broadcast dedicated to showing the paw prints, giving the approximate location of her house, and discussing hunting down the lion with a local game warden. Jenny knows she may be in for a long night. Thankfully, she has the driveway guarded by a sheriff's deputy.

At nine o'clock that night, Jenny hears a noise coming from her carport. She walks over and starts to open the door, then reconsiders. She turns on the carport overhead light and peers through the glass upper door. She sees nothing in the dim light. She goes to the front window of the den. The sheriff's car is gone from the end of her driveway. From the carport comes a "thud". She hurries back to the kitchen door and peers out into the carport again. This time she sees a flowerpot has been knocked off its stand. Movement behind the car catches her attention. She grabs a flashlight from the kitchen drawer nearest the door and shines it at the spot in front of her car. Suddenly, two shiny eyes are glowing in the flashlight's beam. Jenny screams and drops the flashlight, breaking it. Regaining her composure, she once again peers through the door. This time she sees nothing. Jenny rushes to the phone and dials. As soon as it is answered, she breathlessly says, "Michael, can you come here as quickly as you can. I think the lion is on my carport."

"Stay calm. I'll be right there," Michael answers, sounding reassuring.

Jenny is surprised at how quickly Michael drives up. Carrying a rifle, he jumps out of his car. As she watches through the kitchen door's glass, he approaches the house ready to fire. Suddenly he freezes, and Jenny hears him yell at the creature, "Get! Go on; get out of here!"

A large raccoon ambles around the front of her car and off the carport. Michael, with a grin on his face, walks over to the door. Jenny opens it for him to come inside. "Just a raccoon looking for a meal," he says. "Nothing to be afraid of."

Jenny offers him a drink. He accepts a beer. They sit on the sofa in the den and talk of the day's events for a while. Jenny is beginning to feel like Michael may make a trustworthy friend. Their conversation is interrupted by the sound of a pickup truck speeding up the driveway, with yelling heard as the truck screeches to a stop. Michael hurries outside. Jenny goes as far as the kitchen door. She sees Michael talking and gesturing forcefully to a truckload full of men, all of whom appear to have a bottle of beer in one hand and a rifle in the other. After a few more exchanges, the truck starts backing down the driveway. As they pull out onto the highway, several rifles are fired into the night air. Michael comes back inside shaking his head. "Just a truckload of frat boys from Tech come out for a bit of nighttime lion hunting in your woods. Only thing those damned fools would have killed out there is each other. Jenny, it may be like this all night. You really aren't safe here alone. Why don't you come and stay at my house tonight?" This invitation is issued with a smile that warms Jenny's heart.

Jenny hesitates at first while thoughts race through her mind, but then she agrees to go with Michael to his house for the night. She quickly packs a small overnight bag; then they drive off to his house.

Chapter Ten

      Jenny and Michael settle down on the sofa in his living room with a glass of wine. Jenny is surprised at how warm and inviting his living room is. It's furnished with plush leather furniture, elegant draperies at the windows, and expensive accessories throughout the room. Original oil paintings are mounted on each wall. Michael notices her admiring the room. "My late wife did all this. The room is exactly as she had it when she was killed in the accident. I rarely use this room anymore."

      Jenny notices on the far wall a large photographic portrait of Michael standing beside a chair in which a strikingly beautiful, blonde woman sits holding an extremely pretty girl who appears to be about two years old. She wonders if she should comment on what is obviously his late family's portrait. She decides not to mention the picture.

"Your wife had wonderful taste in decorating. Michael, I'm so sorry for your loss. Losing your family in a car wreck caused by an impaired driver is something I understand all too well," Jenny replies as she takes another drink of her wine.

"Yes, we share that in common. At least your parents' killer had the decency to kill himself as well. You didn't have to deal with his surviving." Michael's eyes involuntarily tighten into a squint. Even four years later, his anger bubbles just beneath the surface.

"White Lightning Road seems to have maintained its long history with liquor. There sure were enough people drinking and driving on it today headed for my house," Jenny says.

"Do you know its history? Why it's called White Lightning Road by all the locals, even though on all maps it's simply Highway LA146?" Michael asks. This change of topic sparks his enthusiasm in their conversation, and his anger subsides.

Jenny responds, as she accepts another glass of wine, "Sure I know. Several generations ago people in these parts made moonshine, which they called 'white lightning.' Selling it was illegal, and bootleggers used to make so many runs up and down this road it became known as 'White Lightning Road.' Everybody knows that." She's repeating what she was told, mostly by classmates, back when she was a high school student.

"Wrong! See, what everybody 'knows' can be wrong. You got the part right about moonshiners running hooch up and down the roads around Lincoln and Claiborne Parishes during the 1920's when all these counties were dry by law, but there was no road here then. The parishes' authorities wanted to construct a road running from Vienna in Lincoln Parish to Homer in Claiborne Parish. So, all the men that were arrested for transporting moonshine were sentenced to hard labor building the road. These convicted bootleggers had to cut down by hand all the trees to clear a roadway through the woods, clear the tree stumps and undergrowth, level the ground, burn the debris, and make the road using only shovels and mule-drawn skids. They made it as a dirt road in the 1920's. It was given the name locally as 'White Lightning Road.' It was made into a gravel road sometime in the 50's, I think, and it was finally paved in the 60's. I guess locals will always call it White Lightning Road. They have for some eighty years now, even though sometimes they get the history wrong. Common knowledge isn't always based upon the truth," Michael says, his voice hardening to emphasize his last sentence.

"Well, I learned something new tonight. I guess I'll have to be more careful about believing everything I hear," Jenny replies with a smile.

"Jenny, I'm truly sorry about your parents and even your dog. I should have been friendlier the first time we spoke the other day. I've been so vilified by everyone for the past several years thinking of me as an unpunished murderer that I guess I've lost my social graces. I've suffered so much these past four years, you just don't know…"

Michael speaks with such emotion in his voice that Jenny is touched. She reaches over and places her hand on his forearm; she feels the muscles in his arm tense. Jenny says, her voice barely above a whisper, "I understand how hard it's been. This past year has been a nightmare for me. I'm emotionally and physically drained. Sometimes I don't think I can stand it."

Michael leans over, and his lips meet Jenny's. At first she stiffens; then she begins to kiss him in return, gently at first, then with growing passion. Michael draws her into his strong arms. Their kiss grows even more passionate. Emotions she hasn't felt for fifteen months surge within her. Michael slowly pulls her t-shirt up, over her head, and off. Then his hands deftly slip behind her back to undo her bra. As her bra falls away, Michael leans down and takes her right nipple between his teeth and holds it gently as his tongue caresses it. The sensation drives Jenny's passion and urgency higher. She begins tugging at his shirt; Michael helps her remove it. As she runs her fingers through the hair on his muscular chest, he kisses her with greater passion than before. His hands cup her breasts, and she can feel his manhood stiffening as he leans his body against hers. Michael's hand slides under her panties, down between her legs. He finds her wet and willing. With one swift motion, Michael pulls the panties down to her ankles; then Jenny kicks them completely off. She is naked and ready. Michael picks her up in his arms and carries her to the bedroom.

Chapter Eleven

The next morning, Jenny awakens to find Michael still sleeping the sleep of a tired and well-satisfied man. A slight smile crosses her face as she thinks, *"Well, Sally was certainly right about the panties part."* She slips out of bed, makes a trip to the bathroom to freshen up with a shower, and dresses in a clean t-shirt and shorts. Michael remains soundly sleeping during all her activity. She heads for the kitchen, manages to find his coffee maker and coffee supply, and starts a pot of coffee brewing. She looks around at the kitchen and dining room, taking in every detail. Michael's wife was clearly an adept decorator, and no expense was spared, from the granite countertops to the high-end appliances. The entire home exudes elegance. After looking around a bit more, she wanders into the hallway leading to the master bedroom. Against one wall is a staircase leading to an upstairs room.

Her feminine curiosity aroused, she ascends the stairs and enters the room. It's a huge room that would be any man's dream den, with dark wooden paneling, a pool table occupying the center space, the largest-screen television she's ever seen, and a wet bar along the far wall. She turns and gasps. The sidewalls are covered with hunting and fishing trophies – numerous mounted heads of deer, wild boars, bighorn sheep, elk, and even a moose head are interspersed among mounted bass, trout, and ocean sporting fish. As her eyes scan further around the room, she encounters a stuffed bear in an upright position in one far corner. She turns more to her right and sees in that corner a stuffed mountain lion standing with front paws and mouth in an attacking position. Her mind immediately begins to race. *"Michael has a mountain lion! This man hunts mountain lions. Oh, my God, he could've saved the paws from a kill. He could've made those prints found at my house. After all, he was the one who wet the ground so the tracks showed up. Oh, my God!"* In a panic she turns to leave, but her eye catches a shiny object on the far trophy wall. She walks over to investigate. It's a man's Rolex watch. *"This watch is easily worth $5,000. Why would a hunter have an expensive watch on his trophy wall?"* Then a terrible thought springs into her mind. *"I know who it could have been taken from! My God, I've let a murderer make love to me."* In an absolute panic, she descends the stairs and runs for the door. As she enters the kitchen, she sees Michael; he is standing at the counter in his pajama bottoms, drinking a cup of the coffee she prepared. Seeing her, he breaks into a devilish grin. Jenny comes to an abrupt halt.

"Where have you been? Thanks for fixing the coffee. What would you...," Michael starts, but stops in mid-sentence when he sees Jenny's frantic demeanor. "What's wrong? Did something happen?" Michael's face displays his concern.

Jenny tries to think of something to say to explain her obvious anxiety. Nothing comes to mind. Michael asks again, "What's wrong with you, Jenny?"

Jenny blurts out, "Last night was a mistake. I had too much wine and was too tired to think straight. I've got to get out of here now." With that, she pushes past Michael and out the door.

Michael, now thoroughly confused, calls after her, "Let me drive you home. Let me get dressed. Jenny, wait! I'll drive you home."

But Jenny doesn't want to get in the same car with Michael. She starts for the highway but then realizes that Michael would overtake her in his car in no time. So she alters her course and runs into the woods separating his house from hers. All she can think is that this man is a murderer and she needs to get away from him as quickly as she can.

She hears Michael yell after her, "Jenny, the woods aren't safe," but she keeps running until soon she's deep into the woods.

As Jenny runs between the trees, the undergrowth and grass burrs tear at her clothes and scratch her bare arms and legs. She slows to a walk to avoid getting more cuts and scratches. She suddenly realizes she's never been in these woods. Can she find her way back to her house? Doubts seize control of her mind. She stops and takes several deep breaths. *"Okay, Michael's house is here. My house is a half-mile down the highway from his. I should be able to walk in this direction and find my house."* She tries to hold a mental map in her mind. More confident now, she heads off on what she hopes is the correct line to take her home.

Jenny walks for what she worries is too long a time without breaking out of the woods onto her yard. *"Now I wish I'd done some woodsy things when I lived here before,"* she thinks. *"I've read if you get lost in the woods you'll walk in a big circle."* At that she gives a little laugh. *"How would I know if I were making a circle? All these damned trees look alike to me."*

Jenny is growing tired and exasperated. Suddenly, she catches a glimpse of movement to her left. *"What was that? Was that an animal? Did I really see something, or is my mind playing tricks on me?"* She freezes in position and listens. She hears nothing. She starts walking, this time a little faster than before. She hurries along, looking over her shoulder and to the right and left as she walks. She fights to keep from panicking. Suddenly she can see an end to the woods and the open space of the yard surrounding her house. She's made it home!

As Jenny breaks into her yard, she sees two cars on her driveway. One belongs to Michael. The other is a sheriff's patrol car. Michael stands by the sheriff's cruiser talking to Bobby Yale. Jenny strides straight for the two men.

The deputy speaks first, "Are you all right, Mrs. James? Your friend Sally called in a report this morning that she wasn't able to contact you last night. She was concerned for your safety. But, I understand that you spent the night with Michael here of your own free will. Is that correct?"

"Good old Sally," Jenny thinks. Then she says, "Yes, I spent the night at Mr. Garrott's house. And I found some extremely incriminating things there. He has a stuffed cougar in his trophy room. That means he

could've easily faked the tracks we found in my yard. There probably never was any cougar roaming my woods. He also has a man's Rolex watch hanging on his trophy wall. Ask him what that's a trophy of, why don't you?" Jenny is confident that Michael Garrott will be unable to slip his way out of trouble this time.

Both the deputy and Michael are taken aback by Jenny's outburst. Michael seems genuinely hurt; his head lowers and his shoulders slump. "How about explaining these things, if you can, Michael," the deputy finally asks. "Do you have access to cougar paws that you could have used to fake those tracks you reported? And whose watch is that you've got mounted on your trophy wall? That *does* sound peculiar."

Michael stands silent, with his head bowed, for several long seconds before raising his head to answer. He speaks in a low voice, "Everyone in the parish knows I'm a big-time hunter who takes trips every year to hunt large game. I killed that cougar six years ago on a hunting trip to the northwestern Rockies; it's stood in the corner of my den ever since. Half the men in the parish have seen it there. That is, before they stopped coming to my house four years ago. Ask any hunter who knows me. And the only cougar paws I have are firmly attached to that stuffed cat. Besides, what would be my motive to fake lion tracks in this lady's yard? I'm going to buy the place as soon as she puts it on the market for sale. What would I gain by making people think there's a cougar prowling these woods?" Turning to face Jenny directly, he adds, "I guess I know now why you ran out of my house in such a panic this morning."

Jenny feels her face flush. "Your motive could be to drive me away so you can get this place immediately for some reason. Who knows what hidden motive you might have? And you still haven't explained away the watch." She speaks with conviction, standing erect and jutting her jaw forward.

"Yeah, explain the watch," adds the deputy.

Michael sighs; then he begins to explain. "There's a group of us hunters that meets every year for a big-game hunt somewhere. Where and what we hunt varies each year. One of the guys is a lawyer from Atlanta. One year he got a bit too drunk and bet one of the other hunters in the group that he'd kill the biggest bighorn sheep or he'd give the one that did his new Rolex. He didn't even get a kill! Ever since then, whichever member of the group that gets the biggest kill each year gets to keep the Rolex until the next year. I won it last trip. I don't wear fancy jewelry, so I hung it on a nail on my wall for this year. I can provide you with all the names of my hunting group so you can verify my story."

"This all sounds legitimate to me. I'll let you give me the names and phone numbers of your hunting group so I can check out your story, but I have no further questions for you," Deputy Yale replies. "Anything more you want to ask Michael to explain, Mrs. James?"

"No. Nothing more," Jenny says; then she turns to walk into her house. She stops and turns back to face Michael. "I'd appreciate it if you would stay away from my property in the future, Mr. Garrott. I still think you're a very slick character who cannot be trusted. Everyone might be right about you after all."

Jenny enters her house and watches as Michael talks a minute more to the deputy. They both get into their cars and drive away, and Jenny breathes a sigh of relief at being safely home.

Chapter Twelve

Not long after Michael and Deputy Yale drive away, the telephone rings. Jenny answers it and hears Sally's excited voice. "Finally! Where've you been, girl? You had me worried."

Jenny responds, "I spent the night at Michael's house. I'm fine. I..."

Sally interrupts, "Tell me you did NOT have sex with that man." Hearing no reply from Jenny, Sally continues, "You did! You had sex with him, didn't you?"

Jenny meekly replies, "Yes, I'm afraid we had sex. It was a mistake. I was tired, had too much wine, was feeling sorry for him, was..."

"Feeling sorry for him! Why on earth would you feel sorry for a murderer?"

"Suppose he's not a murderer. Then he's been terribly mistreated by all the local folks for years now. Plus he did lose his wife and daughter tragically. And he's a sensitive man who..."

Sally interrupts once again, "Sensitive man! Jenny, you need to get your head out of your ass. Michael is one slick operator who's not what he says he is. I can feel it in my bones. Trust me on this one."

Jenny huffs, "That's the problem. I'm so confused. I don't know who or what to trust. Michael has a reasonable explanation for everything. There's so much I need to talk to you about. Can you come over right now?"

Sally does not hesitate to answer, "I'll be there in twenty minutes. Put the coffee on."

Sure enough, Sally's car turns in the driveway in less than twenty minutes. Each gets a cup of coffee, and they settle down onto the sofa to talk. "Tell me everything beginning from when I left you," Sally says.

Jenny recounts the details of the past twenty-four hours. When she gets to her and Michael's having sex, Sally demands, "How was he? Was he good in bed? Tell me details."

Jenny feels her face blush. With a grin, she says, "Let's just say sex was as good as I remember it being. Michael does have a good body, and he knows how to use it. But let me tell you what happened this morning." She relates how she found the cougar and the watch in Michael's trophy room, how she fled his house and made her way home through the woods, and then about her conversation with Deputy Yale and Michael. "Michael has a good explanation for everything. He can be so convincing. And he looked so hurt when I accused him in front of the deputy. What if we're wrong about him? What if he's innocent? I could be making a huge mistake with him."

Sally confidently replies, "We're *not* wrong about him. He's too polished a liar to be caught in a lie is all." After a pause, she continues, "What motive could he possibly have to want you off this place badly enough to kill your dog and make you think a mountain lion is prowling around your woods? He knows you'll sell the place to him in only a few more weeks most likely. He'll get the land just by being patient. What could make him be in such a rush?"

Neither woman can think of any motive Michael might have. They sit there pondering the matter; then suddenly Sally blurts out, "Say, how does a man like Michael pay for all those expensive hunting trips to locations all over the world? Why does a man from White Lightning Road run in the same circles as rich lawyers from Atlanta? We need to find out more about what Michael does to earn a living. He doesn't farm. He doesn't have chicken houses. He only has a few head of cattle. He has no job. Where does he get his money?"

Jenny offers, "Maybe he has inherited wealth. Or maybe he married a rich woman. He may not need to work."

Sally says, "We need to do some investigating here. Who can we ask? Hmmm."

Both women sit silently for a minute, each thinking how they might learn more about Michael's financial status. Then it dawns on them who is the most reliable source of information about everyone on White Lightning Road. They look at each other with a look of "Eureka!" on their faces; both women simultaneously exclaim "Bubba!"

They rush to the car and drive to the crossroads store. Six cars and trucks are parked outside. Sally says, "We need to wait until some of these people leave. We need to have Bubba alone when we talk to him. Let's sit here a minute."

Several men exit the store and pass in front of Sally's car. When they see the women inside, one makes a comment neither woman can hear, and all the men laugh and look directly at Jenny. "What do you reckon that was that all about?" Sally asks Jenny.

Jenny replies, "I have no idea. Why were they looking at me?"

Sally shrugs, as she considers the possibilities. "You *have* been in the news a lot lately. You've given the locals a lot to gossip about – all the flap about finding cougars in your woods, your accusing Michael of all sorts of things to Deputy Yale, your having sex with Michael, your..."

Jenny interrupts, "My God, do you think they all know Michael and I slept together last night?"

Sally laughs, "Tongues have been wagging all morning, I'll bet. Once Bobby Yale knew, it was bound to get out. You both are unmarried consenting adults. Nothing wrong with having a little sex; the problem is who you chose to have it with."

Jenny says, "Let's leave! I can't go in there knowing they all know about Michael and me."

"Nothing doing. We're going to talk to Bubba like we planned. We have to get some things figured out," Sally responds. Jenny can see Sally is determined and that it's hopeless to argue with her about leaving.

After several more men leave, Sally decides it's time to go in. The women get out of the car and enter the store. Jenny heads for the milk refrigerator while Sally heads for Bubba. Jenny brings the milk to the counter in time to hear Sally ask, "Say, Bubba, Jenny here got a look at Michael Garrott's trophy room last night. He sure takes a lot of expensive trips for a man with no job. How do you figure he can afford all those trips anyway?"

Bubba studies the two women for a few seconds, then replies, "Trophy room, huh? That's not all you got a good look at from what I hear." He looks directly at Jenny and grins. Jenny's face and throat turn crimson. Bubba continues, "Don't have any idea where Michael Garrott gets his money. He paid cash for his property when he bought it six or seven years ago. He doesn't do any local banking that I know of. Pays cash for everything he buys. He files his own taxes. He uses an Atlanta law firm for all his legal work. Nobody in Lincoln Parish has any idea how much money he has or where he gets it. It must be a bunch though, since he doesn't earn anything locally. It's been a mystery ever since he and his wife arrived. Nobody knows anything about his or his wife's families. Drives the local gossips crazy, it does."

Looking at Jenny again, he asks, "You doing a credit check on your future husband?" He laughs loudly.

Jenny looks down at the floor and says nothing in response.

Sally jumps in again. "Do you know of anything that could possibly make Jenny's property become quite valuable soon? Heard any rumors about oil drillings, new pipelines, a new chicken processing plant being built...anything of that sort?"

Bubba frowns upon hearing Sally's questions. "Something making property along White Lightning Road more valuable? No, not even a rumor of any such thing. I keep hoping for a new Wal-Mart Supercenter across the road from my store, but it ain't gonna happen. This property becoming highly valuable soon...I wish!" Then he asks, "Say, you haven't heard any rumors about something like that, have you?"

Sally leans closer and lowers her voice. "Can I trust you to keep this to yourself?" Bubba nods yes. "Rumor has it that the government is scouting land around here for a new naval base."

Bubba thinks for a second; then he says, "A naval base? Why there ain't no ocean within 300 miles of Lincoln Parish." A quizzical expression crosses his face as he continues processing this new information. "Why'd they locate a naval base here?"

Then, seeing a huge grin break out on Sally's face, he exclaims, "Oh, you were joshing me, wasn't you?" He is still laughing loudly as the two women leave his store.

They return to Jenny's house. Sally says, "If Bubba doesn't know anything about Michael's finances, then nobody in Lincoln Parish must know. Now it's a bigger mystery than ever. I'm going to puzzle about this all night now. Well, I gotta go. I promised Mother I wouldn't be too long. Jody wears her out if she keeps him more than a couple of hours."

Sally leaves. Jenny is now more puzzled and confused than ever about Michael Garrott.

Chapter Thirteen

Late that afternoon the telephone rings. When Jenny answers, she hears Michael say, "Jenny, I really enjoyed being with you last night. I thought we had something special, but I guess I was mistaken. This morning you seemed convinced again that I'm some evil murderer and dog killer who's plotting to drive you off your property. Now I find out from Bubba that you've been asking into my financial status. I'm a very private person, and I want no further contact with you, other than to purchase your parents' property, which we can handle through realtors and lawyers. I won't be contacting you again until then. Goodbye...oh, one thing more. There really is a cougar roaming around your property. Just be on your guard." Michael hangs up before she has a chance to speak.

She sits with the phone in her hand, thinking about the call. Michael sounded so hurt. She could hear the emotion in his voice as though he was truly disappointed by her lack of trust in him. *"He sounds so sensitive! I'm wrong to listen to Sally about him. Maybe he isn't a killer. I'm so unsure of what to believe."*

For the next week Jenny throws herself into the job of disposing of all her parents' possessions. This entails numerous trips to Ruston to donate clothing and household items to Goodwill, as well as frequent trips carrying trash to the dumpster down at the crossroads. Finally, Jenny can see an end to the task.

One morning she telephones Sally. "Sally, I think I'll be finished emptying and cleaning this house in three or four more days. Are you ready to plan our moving in together in Plano? Let's get together later today and talk, okay?"

"Sure thing, Jen. I can come over mid-afternoon for a couple of hours to discuss the move. I'm ready and willing, girl. I've had about all of Mother that I can stand. Trust me," Sally replies with a laugh.

That afternoon, shortly after Jenny has finished eating her lunch, she hears a car drive up her driveway. *"Sally is early. Her mother must REALLY be getting on her nerves today,"* she thinks. However, when she goes to let Sally in, she's surprised to see two men standing there. They are both in their early thirties, well-groomed, and wearing expensive black suits and sunglasses. "Can I help you?" Jenny asks as she opens the door.

One man asks, "May we come in please? We have a matter of utmost importance to discuss with you."

Her curiosity piqued, Jenny nods and opens the door wider for them to enter. "May I offer you gentlemen something to drink?"

In unison both men reply, "No, thank you." Then the man who had first spoken at the door, begins, "Mrs. James, we're agents of the National Homeland Security Bureau, a top secret federal agency whose mission is to safeguard the security of this great nation of ours. I'm agent Brown, and he's agent Jones." As he speaks, each man takes a wallet from his inside coat pocket and opens it to reveal a badge and his picture, then closes it and returns it to his pocket. The man continues speaking, his tone growing more serious. "Mrs. James, your country needs your assistance. National security is involved here. Can we count on you to do your duty for your country?"

Totally shocked at what is taking place, Jenny says, "Are you sure you have the right Mrs. James? I'm Jennifer James. What could I do for national security? You must have me confused with another Mrs. James."

The same man continues, "We have the correct Mrs. James. We don't make mistakes. You are the Jennifer James that has established an intimate relationship with this man, are you not?" With that, he opens his briefcase, removes a picture, and hands it to her. It's a picture of Michael Garrott. "You do know this man, don't you?"

Jenny slowly nods her head up and down as she says, "Yes, I recognize him. He's my neighbor down the road. His name is Michael Garrott. I don't know him all that well, however."

"Well enough to have become intimate with him. Our records show you stayed overnight at his house on the night of August tenth. Is this correct?"

Stunned, Jenny murmurs, "Yes, I guess I did. Why is that any concern of the government?"

The man draws closer and lowering his voice says, "We've had Michael Garrott under surveillance for quite some time now. He's a hard man to gather data on. You're our best chance to get someone close enough to gather the information we need. No one else has ever gotten as close to him in years."

"You want me to spy on Michael Garrott?" Jenny asks incredulously.

The same man answers, "Spy is too strong a word. We just want you to be his companion and pay close attention to his associates and with whom he has communications. Take note of any unusual or suspicious behavior on his part. Your country is asking you to spend as much time in the company of Mr. Garrott as you possibly can. Can we count on you, Mrs. James, to serve your government in this capacity?"

Jenny's mind is racing. She has the presence of mind to inquire, "Exactly what is Mr. Garrott suspected of doing? Is he a spy? Is he a killer? Will I be in danger?"

The men exchange glances. The man who has remained silent up to the present now says, "If we tell you what we know, we would have to kill you ourselves."

Jenny thinks, *"You've got to be kidding with that line. It sounds like something from a B-movie."* However, the man's countenance is serious, without even the hint of a smile.

The other man hurriedly adds, "You'll have to excuse Agent Jones for his attempt at a little agency humor. While we're not at liberty to tell you the nature of our interest in Mr. Garrott, I assure you that he's not a violent man and you'll be in no danger at any time."

Jenny asks, "Do you know if he killed the driver of the car that ran his wife's car off the road four years ago?"

The men act surprised at this question. They exchange looks. The man who has done most of the talking says, "Our agency hasn't had him under surveillance that far back, but I assure you Michael Garrott couldn't murder anyone."

"If I agree to do this...to spy on Michael...how would I make reports to you of what I find?" Jenny's mind is racing, trying to get a grasp on the situation.

"You wouldn't report to us. We'll be in contact with you regularly. You must *never* try to contact us. It could lead to Mr. Garrott's finding out what you're doing. Please remember this: You don't contact us. We contact you."

Jenny thinks a few seconds; then she says, "Michael won't have anything more to do with me. We haven't even spoken in over a week since...you know, that night. I don't think I can get him to see me again. He's quite angry with me."

The man replies, "Surely an attractive young woman such as you can get back on good terms with a man if she really tries. All we ask is that you sincerely try. Will you agree to try?"

Jenny agrees. "All right. I'll do my best. I'll see what I can do."

Both men stand up, shake her hand, and walk to the door. Jenny asks, "That's it?"

"That's all. Do your best to reestablish contact with him, and we'll be in touch. Oh, one more thing. Of course, you must keep this conversation and all your subsequent activities relating to this matter strictly top secret. You must tell absolutely no one. One slip and you could jeopardize our whole operation. Understood?"

Jenny nods yes; then she replies, "Understood. I must tell no one about all this."

Jenny watches the men walk to their car. It's a large, black, new sedan. She stands there, watching as they turn left out of her driveway. Immediately thereafter, Sally's car turns into the driveway and drives up to the house.

Chapter Fourteen

As she is getting out of her car, Sally asks, "Who were they? They looked like they weren't from around here."

Jenny replies, excitement in her voice, "You're NOT going to believe it when I tell you. They were government agents. They want me to spy on Michael for them."

"Spy on Michael? You? What ARE you talking about?"

"They were federal agents who have Michael under surveillance, and they want me to gather information on him for them. Honest!" Jenny can't contain her excitement at this surprising turn of events.

"What agency do they represent? The FBI?" Sally asks, shaking her head slightly side to side as though she doesn't believe what she's hearing.

"No, not the FBI. The National Homeland Security Something Or Other."

"Did they show you their picture IDs with agency badges?"

Jenny puffs up her chest and says, "Why, of course. Do you think I'm stupid? They had proper IDs and everything. They were real government agents, I'm certain."

Sally still doesn't know what to believe. Hesitantly, she says, "Okay. Why are they watching Michael? What do they suspect he's done?"

"They weren't at liberty to tell me that," Jenny responds, "but they did say he wasn't the violent type. They said I'd be in no danger while doing this for them."

"Well, of course they would tell you that. How many volunteers do you think they would get if they told people they might get killed?" Sally says. Then she adds, "Are you going to do it?"

"I agreed to help them. It's a matter of national security somehow. What else could I have done?"

"What exactly do they want you to do? What information are you supposed to be looking for?"

"They said just to be observant. You know, to note whom he associates with and that sort of thing. I'm to watch for any suspicious behavior."

"Sounds strange to me...that our government needs you to gather information on Michael. I thought they have satellites for doing that sort of information gathering. Did you tell them Michael wants nothing more to do with you?" Sally then breaks into a smile and adds, "I've been meaning to ask you, just how bad were you in the sack anyway? One night with you and he wants nothing more to do with you!"

This snide remark reminds Jenny of a detail she hadn't yet told Sally. "Oh, yeah, that's right. I forgot to tell you. They knew that I'd spent the night with Michael at his house. They even knew the exact date."

Sally breaks into a laugh. "Girl, half of Lincoln Parish could tell you that piece of information. Trust me. You don't have to be a government agent to know that tidbit of gossip."

Jenny says, "I have no idea how to get back on speaking terms with Michael. He's plenty mad at me, I believe. Sally, you've got to help me out here."

"Cookies! What man can resist a girl carrying a plate of homemade cookies? Take him a plate of warm, fresh-from-the-oven cookies. Works every time." Sally is beginning to show excitement at the project of getting Jenny back on good terms with Michael. "Michael won't know what hit him. Trust me, girl!"

Jenny's face turns into a frown. "But I've never made homemade cookies in my life. That's what bakeries are for."

Sally's eyes light up. "Mother to the rescue! My mother is famous for her baked goods. You come over tomorrow morning, and we'll make the best damned cookies Michael Garrott ever put into his mouth. He'll *have* to start back talking to you again!"

The plan made, the two women spend the rest of the afternoon guessing what Michael could be doing to be under government surveillance. As Sally is leaving, Jenny says, "Oh, by the way, everything I told you about the conversation with the federal agents and my spying on Michael is top secret. I wasn't supposed to tell anyone about it, but I know I can trust you. You mustn't let anyone else know, okay?"

Chapter Fifteen

Jenny, Sally, and her mother spend the morning in the kitchen, chatting and making cookie dough for both chocolate chip cookies and oatmeal raisin cookies. Sally had explained the night before that Jenny wants to take cookies to Michael Garrott as a peace offering and needs her mother's expertise in the kitchen. As the cookies bake, the women sit at the kitchen table drinking coffee. Sally's mother says, "Jenny, I think it's a nice gesture for you to be neighborly, but you watch out for that Michael Garrott. That man keeps to himself too much. If you ask me, he's hiding something. You know everyone thinks he killed a man four years ago, don't you, dear?"

Just then Sally's father comes into the kitchen to get a drink of water. "You ought not go repeating that gossip about Michael. Everyone around here has him guilty of murder without one shred of evidence against him. No wonder he keeps his business to himself. I would too if everyone thought I was a murderer."

Sally's mother shakes her head, dismissing her husband's opinion on the matter. "Where there's smoke, there's fire, as they say. Michael is so secretive about his affairs that not one soul in this parish knows anything about what he does for a living or where he goes on all those trips he takes. It's not natural to act that way."

As their exchange takes place, the timer dings, indicating the first batch of cookies is ready to be taken from the oven. Jenny gets a hot pad and takes the cookie sheet out of the oven. Just then, Sally's father says, "It's driving you old biddies at the church and all the busybody men at the feed store crazy that someone in the parish keeps his business out of public gossip. It galls all of you that it would take the FBI to learn what you're all dying to know."

There is a loud crash as Jenny drops the sheet of cookies on the floor upon hearing his mention of the FBI. Jenny gives Sally a raised-eyebrow look, wondering if she had let the cat out of the bag. Sally quickly puts her finger up to her mouth and shakes her head 'no' to keep Jenny from saying anything. Sally's mother jumps to her feet to help and asks, "Did you burn yourself, dear? Those pans get awfully hot."

Jenny mumbles, "It just slipped out of my hand. Here. Let me clean up the mess."

In another hour all the cookies are made, and a plate piled high with a mixture of both kinds of cookies is ready for Jenny to take to Michael. "Well, wish me luck," Jenny says as she prepares to leave. "Thank you so much for being so helpful," she tells Sally's mother.

"Call me the minute you get back from delivering them to Michael," Sally says.

Jenny gets in her car and heads for Michael's house. With each passing mile, her nervousness grows, until she reaches the driveway to his house. She turns in, hoping for the best. She parks the car, gets out, and walks to the front door. She sighs, takes a deep breath, and pushes the doorbell twice. She waits a minute; then she pushes the doorbell again, holding it down longer this time. After waiting another minute, she decides to walk around to the back of the house. There she sees Michael digging a hole to plant a bush. He has the hole nearly finished, and his bare upper torso glistens with sweat. As he lifts a shovel full of dirt, his muscles tighten. Jenny likes what she sees and is admiring his toned body when he looks up and sees her watching him. He leans on the shovel and stares at her. She is wearing short shorts and a snugly fitting, low-cut blouse that shows her figure well. Michael keeps staring at her as she approaches and speaks first. "I came to apologize for my behavior the last time we were together. I jumped to some crazy conclusions and acted like a fool. I hope you'll give me another chance." She pauses; then she adds, "I made you some cookies."

Michael stands impassively, staring intently at her for so long that she begins to feel extremely uncomfortable. Finally, keeping a stern expression on his face, he speaks. "What kind of cookies?" At last he smiles and relaxes his posture. Jenny breathes a sigh of relief, and together they walk into the house.

Jenny says, "I hope you can see why I acted like I did. I wasn't thinking clearly. There were so many confusing factors – all the gossip about your being a murderer, the almost ridiculous idea of a cougar being in the area for the first time in thirty years, then finding a stuffed cougar and a man's Rolex in your trophy collection. Then there's the strain I've been under the past year, especially the two weeks before with my mother finally dying and Maxx's mutilation, your pressuring me to sell my place to you…it all just overwhelmed me. But, I really, really like you, Michael, and, if you can forgive me, I'd like a second chance with you…please?" Jenny's expression is both humble and apologetic. She lowers her eyes and the corners of her mouth turn down slightly.

Michael sits silently, mulling over what Jenny has said. Then he responds, "I'm not sure I can go with someone who thinks I'm an unpunished murderer."

Jenny quickly replies, "I swear I don't think that. The sensitive man who made love to me that night could not be a murderer."

Michael's eyebrows rise at her remark. He adds, "And I didn't fake those mountain lion paw prints. As unbelievable as it may seem, there *is* a lion prowling these woods."

Jenny nods. "I believe that now, too."

Michael smiles and says, "I would be willing to give us a fresh start. In fact, how would you like to accompany me on a trip to Shreveport? I'm leaving tomorrow morning to go to the Horseshoe Casino for a weekend of gambling. There won't be so many watchful eyes on us there, so we can be more relaxed."

"That would be wonderful! I'd love to go away with you for the weekend," Jenny says with a smile.

"All right then. I'll pick you up about 10 o'clock," Michael says, sounding pleased.

As soon as Jenny arrives back home, she calls Sally. "The cookies worked! Not only did he forgive me, but he invited me to go to Shreveport with him this weekend. We leave tomorrow morning."

Sally responds, "Good work, girl. You're now officially a government spy. Just you be careful. Don't ever forget he's a threat to national security."

Chapter Sixteen

The next morning, Michael's car pulls into Jenny's driveway promptly at 10 o'clock. Jenny is ready and waiting. Michael loads her suitcase into the trunk, and they get on the road. Thinking about the ninety-minute drive to Shreveport ahead of them, Jenny suggests, "Why don't we take this time to get to know more about each other?"

"Okay by me. What would you like to know?"

"You're a man of complete mystery, so everything. Like where were you born? Where did you grow up? How did you end up living on White Lightning Road?"

Michael is quick to counter the barrage of questions. "Ladies first. How about you starting off?"

"All right. Let's see. I'm a big-city girl from south Louisiana, born and raised in New Orleans, a city I love. The Katrina disaster just breaks my heart. I desperately want New Orleans to recover. My family lived there until I was fifteen; then my worst nightmare came true. My father accepted a job in Ruston, forcing us to move here. Then even worse, he bought the place on White Lightning Road way out in the country. I hated living here and couldn't wait until I got to move back south to attend LSU in Baton Rouge. I loved LSU. That's where I met my husband Randy. We got married right after we graduated. He took an entry-level position with a bank in Baton Rouge, and I found a job at LSU. To help make ends meet financially, Randy joined the Army Reserves. Everything was wonderfully happy until his reserve unit was sent to Iraq. He was killed in action three months later. That was a year ago now. When my father was killed in the automobile wreck three months ago and my mother was critically injured, I came up to stay with her. She died a couple of weeks ago. The rest you know." Jenny turns to Michael. "Now it's *your* turn."

"I'm a big-city boy from Atlanta, Georgia. I lived in Atlanta until I went to Athens to attend the University of Georgia. Go Dawgs! I met my wife Cathy our junior year at Georgia. I loved her at first sight, and for some reason I was lucky enough to eventually win her heart. We got married our senior year at Georgia. Afterwards, we lived in Atlanta, where I did computer software development and was fortunate enough to create a program that was very well received. Cathy was from a small town in the state of Washington and wanted to move away from the big city. Our good friend, the best man at our wedding in fact, was originally from Ruston. He sold us on the idea of moving to north Louisiana. The rest you know."

After a pause, Jenny asks another question. "What was your daughter's name? I saw the family photograph on the wall in your den. She was a lovely little girl. And your wife was beautiful."

"Megan. My daughter's name was Megan. She was two and a half when they died. Cathy was three months pregnant. I lost three people that day," Michael says, his voice almost a whisper. Then he speaks louder. "Sorry. It's been four years, and I still haven't adjusted to it very well."

Jenny quickly says, "I know how hard it is. This past year has been the worst year of my life." There is a long pause in the conversation. Then Jenny says, "I was an only child. How about you? Any brothers or sisters?"

"No sisters. Two brothers, one older who's a bank vice-president in Dallas and one younger who's a lawyer back in Atlanta."

"A lawyer. He must be the black sheep of the family," Jenny says jokingly.

Michael chuckles, then he replies, "No. I'm the black sheep. My brother fits right in. My grandfather started the Garrott family law firm. My father, two uncles, assorted cousins, and my brother are all lawyers. My older brother and I escaped the clutches of their legal empire somehow, much to my father's chagrin."

Jenny comments, "From the look of your trophy room, you must love hunting and fishing. How many trips do you take a year?" She's really fishing for information now!

"I grew up with a shotgun or fishing pole in my hands year around. All the men in my family love both. I guess I average four or five trips each year to hunt or fish."

Jenny thinks, *"This is going so well. Maybe I should ask him about what business trips he takes, where he goes, and what he does on them."* However, before she has time to ask another question, Michael says, "I have it on good authority...Bubba...that you're close to finishing with cleaning out your parents' house and will be leaving any day to move to Plano to live with Sally. When should I expect you to put the property up for sale...to me, of course?"

Jenny searches her mind for a good answer. She can't very well say that the federal government wants her to stay and spy on him. She finally says, "Oh, you know how Bubba can be mistaken about things. I still have a lot of work to do on the house. It may be weeks yet, months even."

"Your parents must have had an awful lot of stuff for you to sort through then," he says. Then he adds, "As much as you say you love south Louisiana, I find it surprising that you're moving to Dallas instead of returning back south."

Jenny explains, "After Katrina's devastation, New Orleans will take years more to return to anything like the city I grew up in and loved, if it ever fully does, and there are too many memories in Baton Rouge. Everything there – my job, my apartment, our friends, the LSU campus, our favorite restaurants, everything – reminds me too painfully of Randy. I just think a new city would help me recover...plus spending some time with Sally should be fun."

"I could never move away from things that remind me of Cathy and Megan. I'll probably live in my house on White Lightning Road the rest of my life." There is an awkward pause in the conversation; then Michael continues. "Changing the topic, what would you like to do in Shreveport while we're there? Anything you would particularly care to do?"

Jenny thinks for a moment; then she responds, "I would love to eat Cajun. They have a couple of New Orleans-style Cajun restaurants in Shreveport – Copeland's and Ralph and Kacoo's. Can we eat at one of these?"

"You bet! We can eat at both, if you wish. You call the shots this weekend."

The conversation continues about what attractions there are for them to choose from in Shreveport. Both are surprised at how quickly the time has passed when they arrive at the outskirts of Bossier City, Shreveport's sister city. Shreveport is a city of approximately 200,000 on the west bank of the Red River, while Bossier City is a city of some 58,000 on the east bank. There are two riverboat casinos on the Shreveport side of the river and three casinos, including the Horseshoe Casino, on the Bossier City side.

As they head for the Horseshoe Casino to check into the hotel, Jenny's mind races with concerns about the upcoming weekend. She wonders if Michael has booked separate rooms for them; she still regrets the night she spent with him and hopes he doesn't expect a repeat of their intimate encounter. It occurs to her, though, that sharing a room would afford her a much better opportunity to keep track of whom he meets and any phone conversations he has. She wonders if Michael has some sort of rendezvous planned; a casino would be the *perfect* place to pass information to an accomplice. It's crowded with lots of people jostling about in close proximity; it's loud enough that conversations are hard to overhear. Everyone is a stranger, so no one recognizes each other. It's definitely perfect for whatever it is Michael does. Jenny suddenly comes to a realization about her new mission. *"I'll bet that's why those agents recruited me this week. Something big must be supposed to happen this weekend."*

"We're here," Michael announces as he stops the car at the front entrance of the hotel. They turn the car over to the valet, watch as a bellhop unloads their luggage, then walk inside and go to the hotel check-in counter. Jenny is impressed at the opulence of the lobby. From its high ceiling hangs an immense crystal chandelier, and a fish tank thirty-feet long containing brilliantly colored fish occupies one wall. They walk to the reception desk, which is topped with a beautiful marble counter top.

"Welcome back, Mr. Garrott. Nice to have you back so soon. Your favorite room is waiting for you," the smiling girl behind the counter says.

"I'll be needing another room as well, please. I brought a friend with me," Michael replies.

Jenny doesn't know if she feels relief or disappointment upon hearing his request. Despite her concerns, she needs to stay close to him this weekend.

"I'm so sorry, Mr. Garrott, but there are no additional rooms available. The hotel is booked solid for the weekend. I could try to find a room in another hotel for your guest, if you wish," the girl says.

Jenny quickly blurts out, "No. That won't be necessary." Then, she turns to Michael and says, "We can share your room if you're agreeable to that." She can tell by the wicked smile on his face that he's agreeable to that idea.

"One room then," he tells the girl.

"Fine. I'll have your luggage taken right up," she answers as she taps the bell for the bellhop.

As they wait, Jenny overhears the clerk next to them tell another guest, "Check-in time begins at three o'clock. We would be happy to hold your bags for you until then."

Jenny thinks, *"Okay, Michael must be a regular here. The girl acts like she knows him, and he's getting special treatment. This must be a regular place for them to rendezvous."*

They ride the elevator to the twentieth floor then follow the bellhop to their room. He opens the door for them and lets them enter first. Their room is spacious and beautifully decorated. There is an enormous king-sized bed, plus by the windows at the far end of the room is a separate sitting area with a sofa and two plush chairs. Jenny thinks, *"One of us could sleep comfortably on that sofa."* After the bellhop places their luggage in the closet and explains the working of the room's thermostat, Michael hands him a tip. "Why, *thank you*, Mr. Garrott. My name is Frank. Please be sure to ask for me should you desire anything further during your stay. I hope y'all enjoy yourselves and win lots of money," the bellhop gushes. Jenny thinks, *"That must have been some tip!"*

"Would you like to try our luck at the casino before we eat? Or would you rather eat first? You're the boss this weekend," Michael says cheerfully once they are alone.

They decide to eat lunch at Copeland's. The restaurant is located across the river in Shreveport in the southeastern section of the city in what has become the busiest and fastest growing part of the city. The drive to the restaurant takes them into lunchtime Friday traffic, and they find themselves still blocks away tied up in bumper-to-bumper traffic. "Now this is a part of city life I *don't* miss," Michael says, visibly getting agitated at the slow going.

Jenny thinks this might be a good time to offer her thoughts on their sleeping arrangements. "About our sharing a room this weekend, I don't...oh, I'm not sure how best to say this...I hope you're not expecting..."

Michael interrupts, "I'm glad you brought this up. I wanted to tell you that I think we should go slow and get to know each other before having sex again. I'm not the sort of man who jumps in the sack with any girl that's willing. You took advantage of my vulnerable state the other night. I'd had too much wine, was thinking about my wife...and the fact I hadn't had sex since her death...and even though what happened was absolutely wonderful...well, I hope you aren't expecting a repeat performance this weekend. While I'm perfectly willing to sleep with you, I won't have sex with you."

Jenny sits there with a look of total surprise on her face. Michael breaks into a laugh and says, "Close your mouth. I just wanted to set you at ease. I want us to relax and enjoy getting better acquainted this weekend. I know you aren't the sort of girl who normally would have sex with a man she hardly knows...Bubba told me." Then he laughs again.

His words have the desired effect. They both relax and are ready for a stress-free weekend.

Chapter Seventeen

Lunch exactly suits Jenny's taste. She devours a Creole redfish and shrimp house specialty dish, while Michael has catfish covered with a cheesy crab sauce. "This reminds me of how I ate all the time down home. I sure love this cuisine," she says at the end of the meal. "How did you like yours?"

"It was quite enjoyable. I would have made a good Cajun. I'm up for anything – alligator, turtle, eel, fish, seafood, armadillo – bring it on," Michael says with a laugh. "I make it a point to try regional specialties in all the different cities and countries I visit."

"Oh, do you travel to foreign countries a lot?" Jenny asks, her interest piqued.

"Not so much nowadays. In the past I spent a lot

of time traveling overseas, especially to Europe."

"Did you travel for business or pleasure?" Jenny asks, thinking she can pump him for information and maybe get clues as to what the nature of the unsavory activity that has him under suspicion by the government might be.

"Strictly for pleasure. Cathy loved traveling. It was one of our favorite things to do together," he replies, as he grows pensive.

"Damn! Seems everything I say reminds him of his late wife. He must have loved her deeply to be so sensitive about her after four years. I need to change the subject," Jenny thinks. She says, "Should we head back to the casino now? Do you play table games or slots?"

"Strictly table games. I do them all – three-card poker, blackjack, craps, Texas hold 'em -- you name it and I'll lose money at it. Ready to go?"

At the casino, Michael sits at a $25 minimum bet blackjack table. Jenny sits beside him but doesn't play. "You're not going to gamble?" Michael asks her.

"At $25 a hand, I'll just watch you. I can't afford that kind of money in one hand."

Michael takes out a roll of $100 bills and offers her several. "Here. Go enjoy yourself on the slots. Watching someone else gamble is no fun."

"I can't take your money," Jenny protests.

"Please take it. It's only money. I print it by the bucketful in my basement at home. I'll never miss it," he replies with a laugh.

Jenny pulls one $100 bill from his hand and heads for the nearest quarter slot machines. She's careful to select a machine where she can watch what Michael does. For several hours she closely watches as various people sit down at the table beside him, gamble awhile, and then depart. Several times a cocktail waitress stops beside him, hands him a drink, and accepts a tip from him. Jenny thinks, *"He could be passing a note with any of these people and I'd never know it. I should stick closer to him."* She walks over to the blackjack table and stands beside his chair.

"How much did you win?" Michael asks her with a smile.

"It took all your money. How are you doing?"

"Oh, I'm down a little over $1,000. But, the weekend is young yet. I hope to win it back and get ahead before we leave."

"A thousand dollars! He's lost a thousand dollars in two hours. He must get a lot of money paid to him for whatever it is he's doing," Jenny thinks.

The weekend passes quickly. It's filled with great dining, lots of gambling, and a few shopping trips to malls in the two cities. Jenny and Michael sleep together in the same bed each night, but they sleep on either side with several feet of space between them. All weekend, Jenny watches Michael's every move but never sees anything remotely suspicious. Jenny loses $300 that Michael gives her, plus $200 of her own. Michael loses $3,700.

On the drive back to White Lightning Road on Monday morning, Jenny asks Michael, "What do you think of President Bush? Do you approve of how he's conducted the war in Iraq and how he's made war on the Muslim terrorists?"

Michael responds, "Let's not ruin a great, fun weekend with talk of politics. Besides, I try to never discuss politics or religion."

The drive home is spent with small talk about the weather and what they enjoyed about the weekend. Michael drops Jenny off at her house. As he is leaving, he takes her in his arms and kisses her. She kisses him back and regrets when the kiss ends. As he drives away, she thinks, *"I could see myself falling hard for him. He seems like such a sweet guy. Too bad he could be arrested at any time for whatever it is he's under investigation for."*

As Jenny watches Michael's car disappear up the road, she hears her telephone ring. She hurries inside and answers it. "Jenny! Tell me everything, girl. Did y'all have sex again? Did you learn anything incriminating? Details, girl. I want details," she hears Sally say.

"No, we did *not* have sex. Michael was totally considerate of my feelings at all times. Sally, I think he's really, truly a nice man, sensitive and gentle. I'm beginning to think the government might be wrong about him."

Sally practically shouts, "Snap out of it, Jenny! He wouldn't be much of a terrorist or spy or whatever he is if he let an amateur like you detect anything suspicious. He may have been living his cover story for years. Don't lose your head, girl. He may still be a killer. Trust me."

"I know. I know," Jenny says. "I can't let myself be fooled by him."

That night the telephone rings. Jenny answers and hears a man's voice. "Mrs. James?"

"Yes, this is Mrs. James."

"This is Agent Brown. I'm calling for your report about the suspect's activities this weekend. Did you establish a good relationship with Mr. Garrott? Do you have any suspicious activity to report?"

"Yes, we got along great. We had a wonderful time together. I didn't see anything at all suspicious. However, he had dozens of opportunities to pass notes with all sorts of people without my knowing, including bellhops, other gamblers, the drink girls. He lost a whole lot of money – about $4,000 all together. He spends money freely. He told me that he had all he wanted because he prints it himself in his basement." Just then, an idea occurs to Jenny, and she says, "Say, is that what you're after him for? Is he a counterfeiter? Could he threaten national security by flooding the country with counterfeit money? Is that it? Is Michael running a counterfeiting ring out of his basement?"

The man says, "No, that is not it! Mike's house doesn't even have a basement. He's not under our surveillance for counterfeiting. Listen, don't be too obvious with your watching him. Don't ask too many questions. Just act natural and encourage him to let his guard down around you. It's important that he gets to trust you. Spend as much time with him as you can. Your country is counting on you, Mrs. James." Then he abruptly hangs up.

Jenny calls Michael. "I sure had a wonderful weekend. I just wanted to thank you again. Maybe we could get together soon."

Chapter Eighteen

Jenny and Michael spend time together nearly every day for the next month. They eat out at restaurants in the Ruston area. They drive to Monroe to shop and catch a movie at Pecanland Mall, the largest shopping center in northeast Louisiana. They take walks in the woods, where Michael points out various plants, insects, animal tracks, and other items of interest. Jenny begins to have an appreciation for the piney woods, which she never cared about previously. And she cares more and more deeply for Michael with each passing day. She makes daily reports to Sally, who has returned to her home in Plano. She makes a weekly report to Agent Brown. Her reports to him are all the same: no suspicious activity. His instructions to her are the same each week: keep close to Michael and gain his trust. Jenny becomes more and more conflicted. As her feelings for Michael grow stronger and stronger, she begins to feel guilty for spying on him for the government. How would she feel if she was the one responsible for his being arrested and sent to prison? But how would she feel if he did something to compromise national security and she might have prevented it by continuing to spy on him? She begins to wish that she never had been recruited by those federal agents.

On one of their walks in the woods between their two houses, they stop to rest in the deep shade under a huge maple tree. Jenny sits with her back to the tree. Michael is reclining with his head in her lap. Jenny strokes his hair as they talk softly. Jenny has been speaking for a while when she looks down to see Michael's eyes are closed. He's fallen asleep in her lap. This sight somehow fills her heart with warmth. She remains quiet and still so as not to disturb his sleep. Soon two squirrels climb down the trunk of a nearby tree and then begin chasing each other around and around its trunk. Jenny smiles at their antics. Suddenly, out of the corner of her eye she catches a hint of motion. As she watches breathlessly, a mother deer and her fawn come out of the thick woods and walk across the small opening twenty yards in front of her. Jenny is filled with a sense of wonderment, like being privy to one of nature's special moments. The deer walk slowly through the open space and all too quickly disappear into the woods on its far side. Jenny realizes that she's actually thrilled to be sitting in the woods of northwestern Louisiana. Never in her life did she expect to have such feelings.

After napping for forty-five minutes, Michael rouses and opens his eyes. Jenny immediately says, "Oh, Michael, it was wonderful. A mother and a baby deer walked right in front of us. It was beautiful. And you missed it."

"I may see them next hunting season," Michael replies nonchalantly, as he sits up beside Jenny.

"What a cruel thing to say! You would kill Bambi?"

"Not Bambi. Bambi's mother during doe season maybe."

Jenny reacts with horror. "How could you be so cruel? How could you kill such a beautiful and gentle creature?"

"Jen, you know I'm a hunter. I hunt game all over the country. You've seen my trophy room. Hunting is not cruel. It's actually performing a necessary function. These woods are overpopulated with deer. They've become a nuisance to farmers; they eat their crops, destroying everything from vegetable gardens to entire pea patches. They even come up to people's houses and eat the flowers in their landscaping. Overpopulation leads to starvation, especially during a drought like we've had this summer. And it promotes disease in the deer. Do you realize that deer have now become a major problem to drivers on the highways here? You never used to see a deer on I-20 between Ruston and Shreveport. Now hitting one is commonplace. Think of the wrecks that causes. The deer herd needs to be thinned each year. Which is more important – a farm family's livelihood and a driver's safety on Interstate, or a deer's life?"

Jenny says without hesitation, "Well, I certainly could never kill a deer." She gets to her feet and starts walking back to his house.

Michael catches up to her. "Maybe you'll let me take you hunting once to see what it's like," he offers.

"Not interested!" Jenny almost shouts, but then her voice softens as she adds, "But you could take me fishing in my father's boat if you would. I'd like to experience that. Dad used to enjoy 'being on the water' as he called it. He was always trying to get me to tag along with him, but I never went."

Michael responds, "I'd be happy to take you fishing. We can use my boat. It's bigger and more comfortable than your father's boat."

"No, it's important to me to use my father's boat. Would you mind?"

"We can go in his boat if you prefer. I'll pick it up from your house today, check it over, and get it ready for the outing. We can go fishing tomorrow. I'll pick you up at your house in the morning at six."

"Six o'clock! I was thinking more like eight or nine," Jenny exclaims. "Six o'clock?"

"Yup. Must be six o'clock. Wear jeans and a long sleeve shirt over your bathing suit, and bring sunglasses and a big-brimmed hat. The sun will be hot by late morning. I'll handle everything else we need," Michael says. She can see the prospect of taking her fishing appeals to him.

Jenny nods in agreement. "All right then. I'll be ready at six o'clock. Geez!"

They drive to Jenny's house in Michael's pickup truck equipped with a trailer hitch. He hooks her father's boat and trailer to his truck and with a cheery, "I'll see you bright and early in the morning, young lady," he drives off. Jenny goes inside to call Sally and tell her all about her experience of seeing the deer so close up.

A little before six the next morning, Jenny hears Michael's truck with the attached boat and trailer crunching up her gravel driveway. She goes outside to meet him. As instructed, she's wearing her two-piece bathing suit under a long-sleeved shirt and jeans. She completes her outfit with the required sunglasses and a wide-brimmed straw hat. They exchange greetings then head for Lake Claiborne located only a few miles farther down White Lightning Road toward Homer. Michael drives into the public boat ramp area and skillfully backs the boat trailer into position for the boat to be put into the water.

"What should I do? Can I do something to help?" Jenny asks.

Michael cheerfully replies, "Just go stand on the pier over there and watch a master at work. And try not to fall in!" Then he backs the truck farther down the boat ramp and into the water's edge, stops the truck, and gets out. He releases the boat from the trailer and climbs into the boat. He cranks the motor and expertly backs the boat off the trailer. He then pulls the boat over to the pier, where he ties the boat to a post, climbs out, and walks back to the truck. He drives the pickup to the side of the ramp area and parks it. Then he returns to the pier and tells Jenny, "While I steady the boat, you climb in and take your seat." Jenny does as she's told; then Michael climbs aboard. He puts on his life vest, tosses Jenny her vest, starts the motor, and heads the boat out into the lake. "Hold onto your hat," he shouts as he gives the gas to the outboard motor and the boat picks up speed until it planes out on the surface of the water. They head directly toward the rising sun. Jenny finds the rush of air past her face and the blowing of her hair to be exhilarating. The sunrise is a beautiful display of colors, brilliant reds and yellows. They speed across the lake until they reach an inlet off the main body of the lake. Michael slows the boat and maneuvers close to the bank. As they slow, Jenny, yells, "That was fantastic! I loved the sensation of flying over the surface of the water. And the sunrise is amazingly gorgeous over the lake. I'm so glad we got to see it."

Michael smiles broadly and answers, "That's why we got here shortly after six o'clock, so you could watch the sunrise from the middle of the lake." He takes a spinning rod and baits the hook with a cricket. Handing it to Jenny, he says, "Let's see you try your hand at fishing. Just press down this lever and throw it toward the bank."

Jenny flips her wrist and sends the cork and baited hook halfway to the bank. The cork floats serenely on the surface. After a few minutes Jenny says, "Nothing is happening. Why isn't anything happening? Maybe my bait is bad."

"Patience, my dear. You must be patient. Just look around and enjoy the scenery."

Just then her cork bobbles, bobbles again, and is pulled under the water. Jenny snatches the line as hard as she can...sending the cork and tackle flying out of the water, over her head, and plopping down behind them in the water on the other side of the boat. Michael laughs loudly. Grinning, he advises, "Try to let the fish have it a few seconds, then pull just enough to set the hook, and reel him in. Don't jerk him clear out of the water."

Jenny gets a few more bites, each resulting in her failing to hook the fish. "This is no fun. They're too hard to catch," she pouts. But then, a fish takes her cork way beneath the surface and, when she sets the hook, she feels a heavy tugging on her line. "I got one! I got one!" she screams as she reels him in. She lifts him out of the water and into the boat. Michael proceeds to remove the fish from her hook. "What is he? Is that a trout? A bass? Or what?" Excitement fills her voice.

"This, my dear, is a bream...and a fine one at that. He's a keeper. He'll make good eating," Michael answers as he places the hand-sized fish into the live well. "Now catch a dozen more."

"Did you say good eating? What, you're not going to stuff him and add him to your trophy wall? My first fish ever?" Jenny laughs, obviously enjoying her success.

She and Michael fish until noon, managing to catch a good number of bream. As the day progresses, the sun begins to bear down hotter and hotter. Although it's late September, the heat of a Louisiana summer has barely faltered. "Are you hungry yet?" Michael asks. Getting an affirmative reply from Jenny, he heads the boat toward shore at a picnic area. They land the boat, and Michael helps Jenny and a basket out of the boat. On a nearby picnic table, he spreads out sandwiches, chips, fried chicken, pickles, and Cokes. "You thought of everything," Jenny says. As they eat, she adds, "Boy, everything tastes so good, even this peanut butter and jelly sandwich."

Michael smiles knowingly. "Food is always better out of doors, especially on the lake." They enjoy their meal and then sit and relax, talking and looking out across the lake. After thirty minutes of this, Michael says, "Time to take your clothes off."

Jenny asks with an impish smile, "What did you have in mind?"

"Why swimming, of course," Michael responds, as he strips off his shirt and pants to reveal his swim trunks. He runs off toward the sandy beach of the park's designated swimming area. Jenny strips down to her bikini and runs after him. They spend the next few hours alternately swimming and sunning on the sandy beach. Late afternoon they pack everything up, take the boat out of the water, and head home.

Jenny smiles broadly as she reflects on their wonderful day. "I had a truly marvelous time today. I never thought going fishing could be such fun. Now I wish I had gone fishing with my father one of those times he asked me if I wanted to tag along with him. Thank you for showing me such a good time, Michael."

Michael smiles and responds, "Sure thing. Glad you had a good time. You never knew you could enjoy the woods and the lake as much as you have the last few days, did you?" He pauses; then he asks a loaded question. "Could you ever see yourself being happy to live here permanently? Or are you still convinced big-city life is the only thing for you?"

Jenny thinks a moment before replying. "I never would have thought I'd say this, but I think I could be happy living in north Louisiana under certain circumstances."

Michael invites her to help him cook the fish they caught for dinner at his house. As they're working in the kitchen preparing the meal, he says, "You must have had time to finish cleaning out your parents' house by now. I'm beginning to suspect that you might be delaying completing the job just so you can stay here."

"Are you ready for me to move to Plano? You wanting to get rid of me?"

Michael smiles at her and says, "No, I'm not. Quite the contrary; I like having you around. I was hoping to hear that you're staying around just because you didn't want to leave me."

"Oh, Michael, I do want to be with you. I could fall hard for you if I let myself."

"Then let yourself," he says as he turns to her, puts his arms around her, pulls her tight against him, and kisses her hard. Passion surges inside her, and she kisses him with increasing eagerness. As the kiss ends, she moans, "Oh, Michael, I *do* love you."

Michael picks her up and carries her to the bedroom. Quickly they are naked and making love with all the passion of newfound lovers.

Afterwards, as they lie side by side, Jenny knows that she loves this man. This prompts her to say, "Michael, I do love you. I just can't let myself be *in* love with you."

Michael turns on his side and, supporting his head with his right arm flexed at the elbow, he studies her face and asks, "Why can't you let yourself love me?"

Jenny turns to face him. "You're still a mystery to me. There are so many things about you that don't make sense to me."

A look of confusion appears of Michael's face. "What are you referring to? What about me doesn't make sense to you?"

"Well, for one thing, your finances. Where do you get your money? You have no apparent means of support? You travel the world. You lose $4,000 in a weekend gambling and act as though it's nothing. And whoever heard of someone not having a checking account? Who pays cash for everything except drug lords?"

Michael lies flat of his back and stares at the ceiling. "All right. If it's so important to you, I'll explain my finances to you. I'm independently wealthy. I sold the rights to the software I developed for thirty-eight million dollars years ago. My brother who's an investment banker in Dallas has increased the value of my portfolio to nearly one hundred million dollars. I can travel anywhere I want or lose any amount I want gambling. It's nobody's business how much money I spend. I do have a checking account with my brother's bank in Dallas. I pay most of my bills on-line. I pay my daily expenses in cash or with a credit card. Cathy and I started doing this when we first moved here because we didn't want everyone in Lincoln Parish to know our finances. Cathy was offended by the nosy questions the realtor and local banker were asking. She figured everyone would treat us differently if they knew we were multi-millionaires. She wanted us to be treated as just plain folks to fit in better. After her death and the driver's murder, without any evidence against me everyone labeled me a murderer. I tried proclaiming my innocence, but they all had their minds made up. I decided to isolate myself even further from the locals' snooping into my affairs. My finances are perfectly legitimate."

"Why didn't you just leave when everyone started thinking you were a murderer? I would have."

"This house was redecorated entirely by Cathy. This is where my wife, daughter, and unborn child died. I couldn't leave here," he says, his eyes now glistening with tears. "Anything else you'd care to ask?"

"Why do you want my property so much? Is it going to become valuable somehow?"

"Valuable? How? I want that property so badly simply because Cathy loved it. If it had been available when we arrived, we'd have purchased it instead of this parcel of land. Cathy loved the lay of your place…a beautiful valley between two hills. Every time we drove past it, she'd say she hoped we'd own it someday. I'm buying it for her." Tears roll down his cheeks. "Anything more you have to ask?"

"No, Michael. That answers all my questions. I'm sorry I had to ask. But, with all those doubts, I could never have let myself love you. I had to know." Jenny softly strokes his chest with her right hand.

Michael pulls her on top of him and kisses her. "Jenny, I hope you can trust me and let yourself love me. For the first time since the car wreck killed my family, I've been looking toward the future instead of the past. I have feelings for you that I wasn't sure I would ever feel again for another woman. Trust me. Love me."

Jenny says, "I can trust you now. And I do love you." But she can't help wondering why the federal government is investigating his activities if what he says is true.

They remain in bed all evening, talking and making love.

Chapter Nineteen

Jenny telephones Sally. When Sally answers, Jenny blurts out, "I love him, Sally. So help me God, I love the man. He's the most sensitive and caring man I ever met. And he has one hundred million dollars." Jenny hears the telephone hit the floor. "Sally?"

Sally retrieves the dropped telephone and says breathlessly, "Did you say he has one hundred million dollars? How did you find that out?"

"He told me so himself. Right after we finished making love. It was fantastic."

"What was fantastic? That he has a hundred million dollars or the sex?"

"Actually, both," Jenny says with a giggle.

"How do you know he's telling the truth? It could just be his cover story, you know?"

"I believe Michael in everything he told me. No man could lie that well. It would be an Academy Award-winning performance if he were lying about this. Besides, I truly love him, no matter what. And I've decided to stop spying on him. I simply don't believe he can be an evil person."

"You better watch out, girl. Sounds like your hormones are overloading your brain. How can you be sure you love him? Y'all have known each other less than two months," Sally cautions.

"I love him. I'm certain of my feelings for him," Jenny retorts. Jenny now has no doubt that she loves Michael under any circumstances.

When Agent Brown calls Jenny three days later, Jenny states emphatically, "I quit. I can no longer spy on Michael for you. I don't care what you think he's done. I love him. I won't help you any more. I can't. I just can't."

Agent Brown responds, "You love him. All right. Our investigation had concluded anyway. I was calling to tell you that Michael has been cleared of any suspicion. He's totally innocent of any illegal activity. He is not, repeat not, now and never has been any threat to national security. We were mistaken about him. Still, your country thanks you for your assistance in our investigation. I hope you and Mike will be quite happy together." There is a pause. Then he adds, "Uh, it would be best if you never mentioned this investigation and your role in it to anyone, especially to Mr. Garrott." Then he disconnects.

Jenny immediately calls Sally. "I told you so! Michael is totally on the level. Agent Brown just told me that they were wrong about him and that he never was involved in anything illegal. I knew it. Michael is for real, and I love him."

"Great to hear it, Jen. Maybe we can all laugh about it at your wedding someday."

"Sally, Agent Brown warned me I should never tell anyone, especially not Michael, about his having been under investigation and about my spying on him. I agree with that. Michael would get angry if he ever learns that I made up with him just so I could spy on him. Promise me you'll never say anything to anyone about any of this. Please, pretty please, promise."

"Sure. Don't worry. I won't mention it to anyone. Trust me."

Jenny is deliriously happy over this turn of events.

Now that Jenny can relax and completely trust Michael, their romance blossoms. Believing completely in your partner is a tremendous aphrodisiac. They become inseparable. He asks her to move into his house, and she doesn't hesitate to accept. They become the talk of Lincoln Parish. They are both blissfully in love.

One day as they lie in bed after an afternoon of lovemaking, Michael says, "You have been invited to attend my cousin's wedding in Atlanta next month. Everyone in the family has heard so much about you that they are insisting I bring you. I think it's time for you to meet your future in-laws as well."

"Future in-laws! Oh, Michael, are you asking me to marry you?" Jenny exclaims, barely able to contain her excitement, as she sits up in bed beside him.

"It does unless you can talk my younger brother into marrying you. He and I are the only unmarried sons my parents have," Michael responds with a smile. Then he pulls a small box out from under the pillow and hands it to her.

She opens the box to find a three-carat, solitaire diamond ring. "Oh, it's beautiful," she gasps as she slips the ring on her finger.

"Is that a yes then?" Michael asks with a wide grin.

"Definitely a yes!" Jenny shouts as she hugs Michael. Then she says, "You realize what a problem you've just caused by giving me this ring while we're naked in bed, don't you? What do you intend to tell your parents…and our future children…when they ask how you asked me to marry you?"

Michael smiles. "My brothers will get the truth. Everyone else will hear how we were walking in the woods behind the house when I got down on one knee and proposed to you."

"You do intend for us to have clothes on in your woodland version I hope," Jenny says with a laugh.

"Why, of course. I'm a gentleman, after all," Michael laughs back.

Jenny kisses him and says, "You have made me the happiest woman in Lincoln Parish."

Chapter Twenty

The next month speeds by. Jenny settles in at Michael's house, and they are exquisitely happy living together. Jenny completes the disposal of the remainder of her parents' possessions and cleans out their house. Michael tells her there's no need for him to purchase the property from her since he'll be acquiring it through merger soon enough. They begin talking about setting a date for their wedding. Before long it's time for their trip to Atlanta for his cousin's wedding. Jenny is nervous now that the day has arrived. She wants his family to like and approve of her. She's so happy that she's grown fearful of something happening to destroy her good fortune. Meeting, and being inspected by, Michael's family intimidates her.

Jenny and Michael's plane lands at the Atlanta airport right on time. They retrieve their luggage, then go outside to be picked up and driven to Michael's parents' house. As they stand by the curb watching for their ride, from behind them comes a loud, "Mike! Hey, Mike!" Michael says to Jenny, "That HAS to be my younger brother. He's the only person in the world who calls me 'Mike'."

They turn around, and Jenny is stunned to see Agent Brown. She's left speechless. Michael hugs his brother, who makes a face over Michael's shoulder at Jenny to indicate for her not to act like she recognizes him. Michael turns to Jenny and says, "Ken, this is my future wife Jenny. Jenny, this is my younger brother Ken." After Jenny stands there silently for a while, Michael says, "Jenny, aren't you going to say hello?"

Jenny manages a weak "Pleased to meet you, Ken." Ken hugs her and whispers in her ear, "I'll explain everything as soon as I can. Don't give me away."

As Michael loads their luggage into the car's truck, Ken manages to whisper to Jenny, "Be prepared. You'll also recognize our cousin that's getting married – he's Agent Jones."

Jenny's mind is whirling the entire time it takes to drive to the Garrott's home. Fortunately, the two brothers keep up a spirited conversation about family news during the drive, and Jenny has only to listen. As they turn into the driveway of the Garrott home, Jenny gets her first view of the house. It's an imposing white, two-story mansion with six massive white columns across the front porch and twin, curved staircases at either end of the porch leading up to the second floor balcony. *"Wow,"* Jenny thinks, *"this looks like something straight out of 'Gone With the Wind.' I'm out of my element here."* There is a long, hedge-lined driveway leading up to a circular drive in front of the house. The house sits on immaculately maintained grounds. The wedding is to be held outdoors on the side grounds tomorrow, so there is much activity with trucks delivering supplies and tents being erected. Jenny becomes very nervous about the prospect of attempting to fit comfortably into the Garrott family. The house is filled with family members preparing for the wedding rehearsal that night. Jenny meets relative after relative until her mind is a blur of new faces and names. She's certain that she appears totally confused to every new relative she meets.

At the first opportunity Ken and his cousin bridegroom hustle Jenny into an unoccupied room and shut the door. Ken says, "Thank you for not saying anything to Mike. Let us explain. As you now know, we aren't federal agents. I'm a lawyer with the family firm here in Atlanta. Pete here is in law school in Athens. We apologize for deceiving you, but we did it out of love for Mike. He'd told our older brother in Dallas about his meeting you and how much you interested him. It was the first time he'd looked at another woman in the four years since Cathy was killed. But then you accused him of all those things, and he was through with you. The entire family has been worried sick over Mike for several years now. He'd made a shrine to Cathy out of the house and property out there. It was all we could do to get him to accompany us on the annual family hunting and fishing trips...and he used to be the most enthusiastic about them every year. We've been worried about his state of mind. He had no plans for the future. He lived in the past. He was chronically depressed. He was going nowhere. We just thought that if you were back in the picture, things might improve for him. We knew you must have been attracted to him. After all, you had sex all night with him before you found the cougar and the Rolex. He really did kill that cougar on a family hunt to the Rockies one year. And the Rolex originally belonged to our Uncle Dave. Mike is a really good guy, and we were just trying to help him out. It seems we were right; you two fell in love with just a little help from us. You aren't mad, are you? And please never tell Mike what we did. He would kill us!"

Jenny is almost speechless. "I'm not mad. Just stunned. We never would have fallen in love if y'all hadn't done this. I just can't believe you fooled me so completely. How did you get the fake IDs?"

Pete says, "That was my department. It's really easy to make a fake ID on a computer these days. Piece of cake."

Jenny adds, "And the badges?"

Pete replies, "Fakes. I bought them at the toy store. They're marshal stars from a cowboy package. $1 apiece. Look, we're all lawyers in this family. We deal with witnesses all the time. We know most people, especially if under stress, can't remember things accurately. We figured you would be so shocked at federal agents in your house that you wouldn't take time to closely examine our IDs and badges. Who questions the authority of federal agents?"

Jenny shakes her head. "And the agency you claimed to work for?"

Ken says with a laugh, "We made up an impressive sounding name. Consuming a few beers helped out a lot in doing that. In fact, we originally conceived the plan itself over a few beers."

Pete adds, "It was hard to keep from smiling while we talked to you. I thought Ken would lose it when I told you we'd have to kill you if we told you what

Michael was supposed to be doing. I forget which movie I stole that line from."

"I think it's sweet that you both care so much about Michael. Not many people have relatives that would go to so much trouble and expense to do what you did. I think I'm marrying into a great family."

Pete says, "Okay now. We all have to swear never ever to tell Michael what we all did. *Never ever.*" They all swear.

The rehearsal dinner that night and the wedding the next day both go smoothly. Jenny tries hard to make a good impression on Michael's family. The night of the wedding, after the reception and family celebration afterwards finally end, Jenny goes up to her room, one of the many guestrooms on the second floor of the Garrott's house. Michael's mother had insisted that she and Michael have separate bedrooms while under her roof. Michael remains downstairs visiting with his father and two brothers. Jenny has changed into her nightgown and is about to get into bed when a knock on the door surprises her. She slips into a robe and answers the door. To her surprise, Michael's mother is standing there with two glasses and a bottle of champagne. "May I come in, dear? We girls have not had a chance to get acquainted yet."

"Of course. Please come in," Jenny replies. The bedroom, even though it's one of the smaller guestrooms, has a sitting area with four chairs and a small table. They take seats, and Mrs. Garrott fills their glasses. Mrs. Garrott still is wearing the formal dress she wore all day and her high heel shoes. Jenny feels uncomfortable being in her gown and robe in her presence. Mrs. Garrott is a dignified-appearing woman – tall, thin and athletic in her movements. She is obviously well acquainted with tennis and golf at the country club. She has regal bearing and impeccable manners. Her long, gray hair is styled in an elegant coiffure with the back of her neck exposed and her hair pinned in place atop her head. After the long day of constant activity, her makeup is still perfect and not one hair is out of place.

"I'd like to get to know more about you, dear," Mrs. Garrott says. "Michael is quite taken with you. He says you are a wonderful person, but he has told us next to nothing about your family background. Where does your family live?"

Jenny thinks, *"She's probably hoping to hear that I come from a family of blue bloods who have been shipping magnates in New Orleans for generations – someone whose family is an equal to the Garrott family."* She says, "My father and mother are both dead. I have no brothers or sisters. My grandparents are all dead. My family consists pretty much of one aunt, who is a nun. We originally were from New Orleans, but my parents moved to White Lightning Road when I was a teenager. Since going off to LSU, I've lived in Baton Rouge. I met and married my former husband there. He was killed in Iraq. Now I have no real family, but my background would be solidly middle class, I guess you'd say."

Mrs. Garrott, sounding most sympathetic, says, "Why, you poor dear, I am so sorry." After a pause, she continues, "Having a large family is one of the joys in life. As a mother, you try to protect your children and ensure their happiness. Michael has a great deal of money..."

Jenny interrupts, "I'm not interested in Michael for his money. I became interested in him before I knew he's wealthy. I'd be willing to sign any pre-nuptial agreement your family cares to draw up guaranteeing I'd receive nothing should our marriage fail." She thinks, *"Lady, I fell in love with your son when I thought he was about to be arrested by the federal government. I'm not after his money!"*

"That won't be necessary. I'm sure that you love Michael for himself and not his money. I was trying to get to the issue of your and Michael's compatibility."

Jenny blurts, "Oh, we have fantastic sex!" Immediately, she thinks, *"My God, I can't believe I just told Michael's mother about our sex life!"*

Mrs. Garrott's expression doesn't change as she continues, "How wonderful for you both, but I had more in mind the lifestyle you each want. Michael has told us that you hate living in the country and originally intended to sell him your land on White Lightning Road and return to urban life, that you wouldn't be happy unless you lived in a large city. You've gotten a glimpse into how the Garrott family lives. Does this lifestyle appeal to you? Is this how you would hope for you two to live?"

"It's not 'me'. I've felt out of place and somewhat awed by this house, by all the talk of golf at the country club, yachting with the yacht club, and having a French villa that I've heard these past two days. I've never known anyone before who owns his own private jet like Michael's Uncle Dave does. But, I would do everything I could to learn to fit in with the family for Michael's sake."

Mrs. Garrott presses, "But do you *want* our lifestyle? Is this how you would choose to live once you and Michael were married and he lets you have your choice of where you two will live?"

"No. I'd prefer a simpler way of life. I want Michael to be happy. I'd live with him wherever and however he wants, be it in Atlanta, in Dallas, or on the far side of the moon."

"And what about on White Lightning Road?" Mrs. Garrott asks pointedly.

Jenny pauses before answering and recalls the past few weeks' activities. "Yes, I could be happy living with Michael on White Lightning Road."

"That's what I was hoping to hear. As his mother, I know Michael would never be content for long after returning to life in the big city. He absolutely detests the traffic jams, the miles of concrete, the crowded shopping malls, and he has little patience with the pretentiousness ubiquitous at the country and yacht clubs. He found his true happiness in life when he and Cathy moved to that house on White Lightning Road. I know he could never be as happy returning to urban life. He loves the woods, his hunting and fishing...he was always the organizer of those dreadful trips the Garrott men take together to go shoot some defenseless creature full of holes...It doesn't have to be on White Lightning Road per se, especially in a house where Cathy's presence is everywhere, but I urge you to keep my son living the rural life somewhere of your choosing."

"Don't you worry, Mrs. Garrott, Michael's happiness means as much to me as it does to you. I don't intend to take him away from what he loves."

"Wonderful! Just what a mother wants to hear. You'll be a lovely addition to our family." Then, Mrs. Garrott shocks Jenny by reaching up and pulling the pins out of her hair, letting it fall to her shoulders. She shakes her hair, then kicks off her high heels, and undoes the buttons down the front of her jacket-topped dress. Pulling another chair in front of her, she props her feet up, pours them each another glass of champagne, and with a smile says, "That feels so much better. Please call me Nancy. I think we're going to get along just fine. Now tell me more about that great sex, and let's talk grandbabies…" They talk for several hours, getting to know all about each other.

On the flight back to Louisiana, Michael says to Jenny, "You and Mother sure hit it off. She told me she expects to attend our wedding soon and offered to have it at their house in the grand ballroom right after Christmas. How does a January wedding in Atlanta sound to you?"

"It sounds wonderful. I'll call Nancy tomorrow to start planning it."

Chapter Twenty One

Jenny and Michael get married in January at the Garrott house in Atlanta. The wedding is a beautiful ceremony with every detail of the wedding and reception afterwards impeccably arranged by Nancy. The wedding guests include two hundred of the Garrott family and their closest friends...plus Jenny's nun aunt and Sally. After their Hawaiian honeymoon, Mr. and Mrs. Michael Garrott return to Michael's house on White Lightning Road. Michael comes to Jenny one day shortly thereafter and says, "Sweetheart, I know it must be hard for you to live in a house decorated by my former wife. I can move on now that you've replaced Cathy in my heart and mind. We can live anywhere in the world that you choose. You just name it – Baton Rouge, Dallas, Atlanta, London, Paris, Rome – wherever your heart desires."

Jenny kisses him and says, "That's so sweet of you. I've been thinking about this also. I've decided there's no place I'd rather live with you than on White Lightning Road. Why don't we demolish my parents' old house and build our dream house on that property? The lay of that land is so appealing."

Soon thereafter they have an architect draw up plans to their specifications and get the construction well started; then they take a three-month tour of Europe. A week after they move into their new home, Michael brings Jenny a gift-wrapped box to open. "What's the occasion?" she asks, shaking the box to guess its contents.

"It's just because I adore you. Open it," Michael replies with a sly grin. Jenny tears off the wrapping and opens the box to find a wooden plaque on which is mounted the preserved bream that she caught on their first fishing trip. The plaque has a gold plate with her name and the date she caught the fish engraved on it. Jenny laughs and says, "This is so sweet. You didn't eat my fish." She gives Michael a kiss; then she says, "Let's go hang this in a place of honor in your new trophy room...somewhere on the wall real close to that ratty old cougar of yours."

The next week, Michael brings her a much larger gift-wrapped box. As Jenny takes it from him, she can feel something moving inside. "What in the world?" she exclaims, until she opens the box to discover a female Pembroke Welsh Corgi puppy that looks exactly like Maxx did. Jenny cries as she hugs the puppy close while it licks her face...and wags its tail stub. "We'll name her Maxxine," Jenny says softly.

A few weeks later, Michael finds cougar tracks in the woods behind the house. He tells Jenny, "You won't believe this, but that cougar is back prowling the woods again. I'd better try to kill it before it gets hold of one of our calves...or Maxxine."

"Must you kill it? Can't you just scare it away? It's probably either old or crippled. I hate to think about you killing it."

Michael's face registers surprise at Jenny's words. "After it killed Maxx, I thought you wanted it dead. Why have you now changed your mind?"

"I did want it killed back then, but now it seems a shame since it played a role in our getting together. Besides, it's just being what nature made it."

"All right, if you wish, I'll see if I can handle this without having to kill it."

Michael makes inquiries with the local game wardens and is put in contact with an eastern Texas wildlife preserve that accepts big cats to live out their lives in comfort. A few days later, two men from the preserve arrive and set up in the woods a cage-style trap baited with a calf the mountain lion had killed the day before. Two days afterwards, the lion is caught. The lion is sedated and moved to a cage on the back of the preserve's pickup truck. It turns out to be an old, arthritic male, which explains why it had taken to hunting calves, sheep, and pets near human dwellings. After dismantling and retrieving their trap from the woods, the men load it onto a second truck; then they prepare to leave. Jenny comes out to get a closer view of the cougar. It backs into a corner of the cage and, with its ears laid flat against its head and its teeth exposed, it emits a long, low growl. Jenny examines him; then she remarks, "Poor thing. Your ribs are showing. You look half-starved." The cougar closely watches Jenny with his large, yellow eyes fixed in an unblinking stare.

One of the men from the wildlife preserve says, "This old fellow has had a hard time of it. The woods are full of deer, his main prey, but he's too old and slow to kill them anymore. It's kind of like he's been in the ancient mariner's situation of water, water everywhere and not a drop to drink. So, he's been forced to kill what he can still catch, which unfortunately includes farm animals and people's pets. But now he'll live out his life with us and never go hungry again. His hunting days are over."

As the two trucks turn onto the road and head back to Texas, Jenny and Michael watch; they stand with her arm around Michael's waist and his arm around her shoulders. "Thanks for not killing him, Michael. I feel much happier knowing he'll be well taken care of in his old age. I feel so sorry for him!"

Michael replies, "As long as he's out of our woods, I'm satisfied...although he'd have looked pretty good stuffed and standing in the corner of my trophy room next to my other cougar." He smiles as Jenny looks at him with a frown; she pokes him in his ribs and walks inside the house, with a laughing Michael close behind.

Over time, Jenny convinces Michael of the need to become closer with their neighbors in Lincoln Parish. They host several barbecues which hundreds attend. Soon, Jenny has a circle of women whom she meets for shopping outings and luncheons, while Michael has no shortage of hunting and fishing buddies. That way they are able to keep current on all the local gossip...

Ten months after their marriage, at the birth of Jenny and Michael's first son, Sally stands beside

Michael as they peer through the hospital nursery's window at his newborn boy. "Have you picked out a name for him yet?" Sally asks.

Michael answers, "Jenny wants to name him Kenneth Peter Garrott. I argued with her that our family already has both of those names represented, but she won't budge."

Sally smiles knowingly and says, "That's the perfect name. Trust me."

Part Two

~

Sally's Story

Chapter One

Three days after the birth of Kenneth Peter Garrott, Jenny brings him home from the hospital in Ruston. Jenny is the happiest she's ever been. The past year has been the most wonderful year she could possibly imagine – she married a man she loves deeply, and he happens to be a multimillionaire; they had the house of her dreams constructed; they honeymooned in Hawaii and then toured Europe; she has adjusted to life in the country and has numerous new friends; and now she has given birth to a son. Jenny and Sally sit together on the back patio enjoying the mild October afternoon. The sunshine is bright and warm. A gentle breeze stirs the fall foliage with its yellow, red, and orange decorations. Jenny says, "You know, Sally, back when we were in high school, I would never have thought I'd ever say this...but I can't imagine myself being happier living anywhere else in the world than in this house on White Lightning Road. Look how gorgeous the woods are right in my back yard. It took me a while, but I've come to love these woods."

Sally smiles. "You've definitely been converted. But then, things here are just about perfect for you. I'm truly happy for you, Jen. You have everything a girl could hope for, especially Michael. A man that is loving, considerate, sensitive, AND rich for a husband. I want one!"

"Speaking of wanting a husband, you haven't mentioned in months how your dating is going. What happened with that last guy?"

"George? He turned out to be as big a jerk as all the rest I've had dates with since the divorce. I've kissed a lot of frogs in the past year without finding one prince. My lips stay coated with frog slime. It seems men these days only want to hook up. They expect sex on the second date, if not the first. And you should see how they run when they find out I am a single mother with a five-year-old son. It's like trying to attract Superman while wearing a dress made of kryptonite. And even if they do remain interested, it's difficult for me to have a relationship. I refuse to let a man stay overnight with Jody there, and Jody can't be left alone. I've about given up all hope of finding a man." Sally's face grows more serious as she continues. "Eric is being a bastard again." Eric Jeffers is Sally's ex-husband. After their divorce, he immediately married his pregnant mistress, and they now have a daughter. "He keeps asking me who I'm dating. He asks Jody if there are men coming around and if they 'sleep with mommy all night and are there in the morning.' He threatens me that he'll go to court and seek custody of Jody if I have men in the house overnight since it would be a bad environment for Jody. He's doing it just to harass me. He seems to want to keep me stressed out. It's easier just to not try to date anyone right now. Besides, work and Jody take up all my time anyway."

Jenny says sympathetically, "Hopefully things will improve for you soon. We need to get you back in the game again, girl."

The following Monday morning, after Sally has returned that weekend to Plano and to her job as executive secretary to the regional manager of the Dallas office of a national insurance company, Sally calls Jenny from work. "You're not going to believe this, Jen. When I returned to work this morning from last week's leave, I walk in to find that my boss has been promoted to vice-president and will be transferring to the home office in Atlanta. And, get this, he wants me to go with him as his personal secretary. He says he can't make the move without me there to help him transition into his new duties. Oops, gotta go. I'll call you tonight after work."

Jenny waits all day for Sally's call. Finally, after eight o'clock, Sally is on the telephone. Jenny inquires, "Are you seriously considering moving away from Plano? Give me the details. Could you see yourself actually leaving Dallas?"

"It's a done deal! I accepted already. Jen, it was too good to refuse. The company will pay my moving expenses and relocation costs, including my first two months' rent. My salary will be substantially higher. I'll be able to afford better things for Jody. Not to mention I'll get away from Eric and his harassment. I had to do it. Now I'm getting excited. I'm moving to Atlanta!"

"Wow, I'm stunned. That sounds like a fantastic deal. Say, you haven't been fooling around with your boss, have you?" Jenny asks with a laugh.

"No, it's nothing like that. Mr. Burke is a happily married man, in his forties, with three children. There's been nothing of that nature between us ever. You just never realized how efficient a secretary I am. We have a strictly business relationship. Trust me."

"Well, you have my very best wishes for this move to turn out great for you. It sounds like it could be the answer to your problems. When will you make the move?"

"At the end of the month!" Sally is practically bursting with excitement over this new turn of events.

Chapter Two

The move to Atlanta goes smoothly, and Sally quickly gets settled into her new apartment, which is convenient to her new job. She enrolls Jody in kindergarten and finds a nearby after-school program for Jody to attend until she gets off work. Much to Sally's relief, Jody immediately likes both his school and his after-school program. After getting settled, Sally reports for orientation and training at her new position, while her boss Sam Burke takes another two weeks off work to get his family moved into their new country club home. Within a few weeks of her arrival in Atlanta, Sally already feels at home.

During orientation Sally meets a number of other secretaries and soon learns the network of secretaries and assistants throughout the headquarters. Due to her position as personal secretary to a company vice-president, Sally ranks high in the hierarchy, which makes her a popular lunch companion for the younger, entry-level secretaries. Today two girls from the secretarial pool invite her to join them for lunch at The Varsity, the Atlanta shrine to fast food dining. As they walk into the North Avenue Varsity, an immense restaurant covering two blocks, Sally is struck by its size and its hustle and bustle. As the world's largest drive-in restaurant, eight hundred diners and six hundred vehicles can be accommodated at maximum capacity. Cries of "What'll ya have? What'll ya have?" come from behind the counter. The line moves quickly, and the three women soon are served. Sally gets a chilidog, onion rings, and a frosted orange drink. The women find seats in one of a series of rooms, each featuring its own television. They choose seats in a room where ESPN is playing. "Best room to meet Tech boys," one of her companions says about the room, obviously hoping she'll attract the eye of a student who is here for lunch from the nearby campus of Georgia Tech.

"Now I know why you two chose this place for lunch," Sally laughingly says. "I'm too old to be interested in college boys; so any we see are all yours." The situation makes Sally acutely aware of her age. At twenty-nine, she has little in common with her nineteen- and twenty-year-old lunch companions.

"This place is an Atlanta landmark! Everyone eats here. We thought you should be introduced to one of Atlanta's institutions is all," the older of her companions answers.

As they chat and eat their lunch, three boys wearing Tech shirts at a nearby table stare at them. Then one of the boys nods and smiles. Sally's companions smile back, and the boys get up and come sit beside them. "Ladies, may we join you?" one of them asks, sitting down next to one of the girls without waiting for a reply. Quickly, they are paired off and talking as couples. The conversations of the other two pairs are lively and interspersed with laughter. Sally and the boy next to her sit eyeing each other. Finally, he says, "I can tell you and I are going to become close friends. All of my close friends call me 'Stud'."

Sally laughs, shakes her head side-to-side, and responds, "That is one of the worst pick-up lines I have ever heard. Does that *ever* work?"

"No, not really...Let's start over, Red. I'm Bill Morris, and I really do hope we become close friends," he answers, then smiles warmly.

Sally thinks, *"He's really quite cute. Too bad he's so young."* She says, "My name is not Red, it's Sally, and we will *not* become close friends. Trust me."

"You might be surprised if you give it a chance. I can be adorable. Why not let me have your phone number, and I'll call you about getting together this weekend?"

Sally frowns; then she says, "I'm sure you must have a class to get to, and we need to get back to work." Turning to her companions, she announces, "Ladies, we really *must* be going now." She stands up, ready to leave. The other two women are less eager to depart; however, they reluctantly agree and rise to leave, but only after giving their new acquaintances their cell phone numbers.

On the way back to work, the younger girls talk excitedly about meeting the boys and about the prospect of going on a date with them. Sally wonders if she was ever that young and foolish.

The next Saturday morning, Sally takes her week's laundry to one of the apartment complex's laundry rooms conveniently located two doors away from her ground floor apartment. She is in luck, finding enough empty washers to hold all of her and Jody's dirty clothes. She starts all the washers and goes back to her apartment, where Jody is watching cartoons on television. She returns to change the loads of wash to the dryers. Then, in an hour, she brings Jody with her while she folds their clothes using the large tables provided. She carefully folds all of Jody's clothes and begins folding hers. As she holds up a pair of her panties to straighten them out for folding, a voice behind her says, "Somehow I just knew you'd wear sexy undies, Red." Sally turns around to face the boy from The Varsity. Surprise fills her face. He continues, "I didn't know you lived here. I thought I knew all the girls here, and I've never seen you here before. This must be fate."

She stammers, "We just moved here from Dallas. You live here then, do you...uh?" She can't remember his name. All she can recall is Stud.

"Bill. Bill Morris. We met three days ago at lunch, remember?" He frowns in disappointment that she forgot his name. He definitely remembers hers.

"Right. Bill. You don't live on campus?"

"No. I live here with my two roommates. You met them earlier as well. How about going to a movie with me tonight? It seems predestined that we spend time together tonight. We mustn't tempt fate."

"Look, Bill. I have a five-year-old son. I'm too old for you. My having a relationship with you is out of the question, so why waste your time? Besides, there's no way for me to find a babysitter."

"How old are you anyway? You don't look so old."

"I'm twenty-seven," Sally lies, knocking two years off her true age. "How old are you? Twenty?"

"No, I'm twenty-three. Four years difference in age isn't enough to matter. So, how about you go out with me?"

"It would never work. Sorry, " Sally says firmly. She gathers her laundry, and she and Jody return to their apartment.

Chapter Three

      Sally thinks about Bill throughout the afternoon. She feels flattered to have attention paid to her by any man, even one younger than she. *"If only he were older! He's really cute and seems nice,"* she keeps thinking, *"but he's too young and inexperienced for me. He's still in college, for Christ's sake."*

      Shortly after five o'clock there is a knock on Sally's door. She opens the door to find Bill standing there; he's grinning and holding two large grocery bags. "May I come in?" he asks.

      Sally stays immobile. "How did you find me? I never told you where I live." Her face is stern, and her eyes narrow.

"Hey, I'm not stalking you. I saw you come here from the laundry room. It's only two doors away. How could I *not* have noticed where you live?" Bill replies defensively.

"What's in the bags?"

"If you let me in, I'll show you."

Sally relents and opens the door for Bill to enter. He walks to the kitchen table and removes items from the first bag. "I brought supper. For your son I have chicken nuggets, fries, and chocolate milk. For us I brought hamburgers, onion rings, and Cokes. I even bought donuts for dessert. Smells good, doesn't it? Aren't you hungry?"

Jody comes over to investigate. He is unsure of just who Bill is, but he is sure he would like the supper he brought. "Mom, can I have it? He got it for me. Can I have it?" he shyly asks Sally.

Sally considers for a moment as both Jody and Bill look at her hopefully. "All right. It would be a shame to waste food. Let's eat," she finally says. Jody lets out a cheer. Bill smiles and begins unwrapping the packages and opening the boxes. While they all enjoy the supper together, Bill talks to Jody primarily, only occasionally directing his comments to Sally. Jody has warmed up to Bill considerably by meal's end.

As Sally clears away the trash from the table, Bill announces, "Bag number two contains after-dinner enjoyment. Movie, anyone?" He takes out several cartoon movies, including 'The Lion King' from the bag. "Jody, which would you like to watch with me?"

Jody exclaims with excitement in his voice, "Lion King! Lion King! Mom, look, he brought Lion King!"

Sally smiles. "That's his favorite movie ever. How'd you know to rent that one?"

"Lucky guess. My two older sisters have kids, and my nephews are around Jody's age. They love this movie; so I took a chance Jody would also."

Sally puts the DVD into the player, and she and Bill sit together on the sofa while Jody sits on the floor in front of the television. As they watch the movie, Sally can feel Bill glancing often at her out of the corner of his eye. At the end of the movie, Bill says to Jody, "Must be time to have a snack, brush our teeth, have a bath, read a book, and go to bed, eh? How about a donut for a snack...if it's okay with your mommy?"

Sally is impressed. "You know the bedtime routine for a five-year-old pretty well. That is how we do it around here – minus the donut!"

"I told you, I have several nieces and nephews. I've helped out with getting them into bed from time to time. So, Mom, can he have a donut for his bedtime snack just this once?"

"Only half. He doesn't need that much sugar right before bed."

Turning to Jody, Bill says, "A little boy can *never* have too much sugar, can he, tiger?" He tickles Jody's ribs; Jody laughs and reaches for the donut.

After his snack is consumed, Sally helps Jody with brushing his teeth and taking his bath. Then they return to the living room for Jody to say goodnight to

Bill. Afterwards Sally takes Jody to his room, reads him a book, and tucks him into bed. She returns to the living room to find the lights out, with candles burning on the tables at each end of the sofa and an opened bottle of wine with two glasses sitting on the coffee table. "You have your choice of movies, milady, from 'Sleepless in Seattle', 'When Harry Met Sally', or 'An Affair to Remember.' For refreshments, I offer you microwaveable popcorn and M&Ms," Bill says with the flair of a maitre d'.

Sally looks around at all he has done; then she asks, "White or red wine?"

"Red, milady."

"Then I'll have one of those delicious-looking donuts. I find donuts go better with red wine than popcorn. And you may show 'Sleepless in Seattle'," Sally says, matching his exaggerated flair in her voice.

They watch the movie and drink the wine. By the time Meg Ryan meets Tom Hanks on the roof of the Empire State Building at movie's end, Sally is crying on Bill's shoulder. Realizing the time, she sits up and dries her eyes. "Unless you have something more in those bags of yours, I need to call it a night. Jody gets up early, even on weekends. I enjoyed tonight though. Thank you for a truly lovely evening," Sally says as the movie credits roll.

"I had a wonderful time, too. I told you we were meant to watch a movie together tonight. Now you see that we can be friends, even if you are an old woman."

Sally hits him on his shoulder. "That's *older,* not old." They both laugh. Sally walks Bill to the door, half expecting him to try to kiss her. Instead, he simply smiles at her and leaves with a "See you later, Red." She feels disappointment at his departure.

Lying in bed that night, Sally reviews the events of the evening. She thinks about how good Bill was with Jody, how thoughtful Bill was, how enjoyable and special the night had been, and how nice it would be if only he wasn't so damned young.

Chapter Four

Sally doesn't see Bill again until the following weekend. Since it's Thanksgiving, she has both Thursday and Friday off work for the holiday. Sally spends Thanksgiving Day alone with Jody. They eat out for their holiday meal, and she places telephone calls to her parents and to Jenny back on White Lightning Road. Being so far from them on the holiday makes her depressed. On Friday around noon, Sally answers a knock on her door to find Bill standing there smiling. "Can Jody come out to play?" he asks in a small-boy's voice. "You, too, if you wanna. We could go to the park."

"Why, hello, Bill. I wasn't sure when I'd see you again. I wanted to tell you I really enjoyed last Saturday, but I haven't seen you around all week."

"It was a busy week. I had to study for three tests

the first of the week. Tech is a hard school, especially senior year. I don't ever have much free time during the week, but it was worse with the holiday this week. Then yesterday I rode down to Macon to spend Thanksgiving with the family of one of my roommates. But, I'm awfully glad you missed me." Bill breaks into a wide grin.

They get Jody and head for the parking lot. "It'd be easier if we take my car," Sally says. "It has Jody's car seat in it."

"Sure thing! Taking your car is better anyway. I drive a piece of crap -- an old Honda Civic. It can be rather unreliable."

At the park, they sit at a picnic table, talking as they watch Jody play on one piece of playground equipment after another. Finally, Jody tires and settles into a sandbox to build sandcastles. Bill suggests that he and Sally "shoot a few hoops" on the basketball half-court next to the sandbox. "We can keep an eye on him while we play a game of horse." They each shoot a few warm-up shots. Bill chides, "You shoot like a girl. I'll spot you the h-o-r, and I'll even shoot all my shots left-handed. We'll play the best three-of-five, and the loser has to cook supper for the winner."

Noting that Bill has shot all his warm-ups right-handed and not liking his cockiness, Sally agrees to the match. Bill easily beats her three quick games of horse, making left-handed long shot after long shot with ease. "What's for supper?" he asks as the ball swishes through the net for the winning 'e'.

"How about salad, steak, and baked potato?"

"Sounds fine. A manly meal fit for a jock such as I," he responds with a hearty laugh, puffing up his chest in an exaggerated display of manliness.

"If you thump your chest like Tarzan, the deal is off," Sally says. However, she actually finds his actions amusing.

They stop by the grocery store on the way back to the apartment complex; then Sally prepares their supper. As they are eating, Sally notices Bill is holding his knife in his left hand to cut his steak. When she comments on this, Bill says, "Of course I cut using my left hand. I'm left-handed. I just happen to shoot all my warm-up shots on the basketball court right-handed before I make a bet." He laughs first, but Sally soon joins him in laughing over being taken in by him.

"Humph. I can see I'll have to watch myself around you. You're a clever little devil."

"Not little...just overly young," Bill corrects playfully.

After supper, Bill leaves. Once again he makes no effort to show any affection. Once again it's "See you later, Red."

Jenny calls later that night. Sally casually mentions she is "sorta" dating a Tech student. Jenny barrages her with, "A college student? Is he legal? He's at least eighteen, isn't he? Is he a freshman? What *are* you thinking, girl?"

Sally gets defensive. "He's a senior. He's twenty-three; so there is only a four-year difference in our ages. I'm *not* robbing any cradles here. And, besides, we're just friends. He hasn't even tried to kiss me."

"Four years? Who are you trying to kid? I know you're twenty-nine. He may only be six years younger, but I'll bet he's had a lot fewer life experiences than you. He sounds too young for you, Sally. You need to keep your head together," Jenny warns.

After their conversation, Sally knows Jenny is right about this situation, but she still feels annoyed at her advice. Then the telephone rings again. It's Bill. "How would you like to go to the Georgia Tech versus University of Georgia football game with me tomorrow? Two tickets on the forty-yard line just fell into my lap. It would be fun. How 'bout it, Red?"

"I'm not much into football. And I'd have to try to find a sitter for Jody...but okay. I'd like to go."

"Great! You arrange a sitter, and I'll pick you up at eleven. We'll grab a bite at The Varsity before the game and have plenty of time to be seated before the kickoff. See you tomorrow!" His call restores her happy mood.

Sally arranges for the neighbor above her, a woman in her fifties whose own children are adults now, to watch Jody. "It will be a treat for me. Just like spending time with one of my grandchildren. Stay out as long as you like," the lady says.

Sally and Bill have a pre-game lunch at The Varsity as planned. It's even more hectic than the first time she was there. It seems half the people attending the game had the same plan as they, but service is quick and they find a seat easily. Afterwards, when they enter Georgia Tech's Bobby Dodd Stadium, Sally is immediately impressed at the sheer size of the crowd. "There must be 60,000 people here," she exclaims.

"Close to that," Bill replies. "Haven't you ever been to a college football game before?"

"Once. When I was in high school, my parents took me to a Louisiana Tech game. But it was nothing like this. That stadium was much smaller, maybe half this size."

"Welcome to big-time collegiate football! We are in the ACC, and Georgia is in the SEC. Both are premier conferences. Georgia is ranked in the Top Ten again, but we have a good team and may be able to upset the Dawgs. It'll be a spectacle in any case if you've never seen it before. It's a huge intrastate rivalry, and both teams really hate to lose this game," Bill explains. "Sit back and take it all in."

Sally spends her time gawking at the ever-increasing crowd, watching the two teams come on the field for their pre-game warm-ups, and then enjoying the bands performing. She feels the crowd grow tense at the kickoff. The roars and moans of the fans delight her. Soon she is on her feet yelling whenever Tech makes a good play and groaning when they fail to. The Georgia team dominates the first half, and the Tech fans grow restless as their disappointment grows. Bill seems to be enjoying watching her more than the game. Every once in a while she catches him looking at her and smiling. The performances by each band at halftime fascinate her. Bill leaves to use the restroom and buy them some Cokes. He misses most of the halftime. The third quarter sees Georgia score twice more, making the score as they enter the fourth quarter 31 to 3. Midway through the last quarter, Tech fumbles again, and Georgia has a quick scoring drive. It's as if someone flipped a switch. Fans begin leaving in droves. "Where's everyone going? The game still has eight minutes left," Sally asks.

Bill shakes his head and replies, "It's as good as over at 38 to 3. Why don't we go, too? I can show you around campus."

Sally reluctantly agrees. She's still having a wonderful time at the game. However, she soon is enjoying the tour of campus equally well. For the first time in her life, she regrets that she never got to attend college.

When they return to her apartment, Sally thanks her neighbor for staying with Jody; then she invites Bill to stay for supper. She prepares spaghetti with salad and garlic bread. When she enters the living room to call them to supper, Sally stops at the doorway and watches Bill wrestling on the floor with Jody, who is squealing with delight. Finally, she says, "I hate to interrupt, but supper is getting cold." Both jump to their feet and head for the kitchen.

Later that night after Jody has been put to bed, Bill prepares to leave. At the door, Sally says, "I had an absolutely marvelous day with you today. Thank you for making it so wonderful. I don't remember when I've had such a fun day."

Bill leans toward her, takes her in his arms, and kisses her tenderly. The kiss becomes more passionate as Sally responds. Sally feels her knees start to buckle. At the kiss's end, Bill says, "Red, I think it's time we start to officially date."

Sally manages a weak "Okay" as he walks away.

Chapter Five

Bill and Sally spend all day together on Saturdays and Sundays for the next three weeks. In addition, on one or two weekdays each week, they eat supper at the fast food restaurant of Jody's choice. They are swiftly becoming a couple, one that kisses often and well. At Christmas, Bill goes home to Boston to spend the Christmas break from school with his parents and family. This is Sally's ex-husband's turn to have custody of Jody for Christmas. According to the terms of divorce, each parent has custody for any particular holiday in alternating years. Sally had Jody on Thanksgiving this year, so her ex-husband gets him on Christmas. Sally and Jody fly to her parents' home on White Lightning Road for the holidays. Her ex-husband picks up Jody from there for three days, the 24th, 25th, and 26th. Sally enjoys Christmas Day with her parents, but she misses Jody terribly. Jenny invites Sally to spend the afternoon with her and Michael on the 26th. The two women sit in the den talking, catching up on all the happenings in their lives.

"Jen, I really think I'm falling in love with Bill. He's so sweet, and he's really good with Jody. I'm beginning to fall for him hard. I think we can make this work. I really plan on trying to," Sally confides.

Jenny grows thoughtful. "Sally, you know I want you to be happy and that I always wish the best for you in life, but do you really think this will work? He's *so* much younger than you."

Sally bristles. "Why is it no one thinks anything about the man being ten or fifteen years older than the woman, but let the woman be only six years older than the man and it's a big deal? Take you and Michael. He's seven years older than you. Bill is only six years younger than I am. What's the difference?"

"The difference in this case is more experience than number of years. Bill is still in college. He knows nothing of life but being in school. You've lived your twenties by getting married and divorced twice, working, and raising a son. You're at a much different place in your life than Bill is. That's all I'm saying. He's much younger not in age so much as in living."

"Jen, I want this to work. I'm going to make it work. Bill will graduate in late May, and he can get a good-paying job as an engineer. We could be happy together. I know we could."

"All right then. I know just what you need. For once, you trust me. I'm taking you to Shreveport tomorrow. Put yourself in my hands."

The next day Jenny drives Sally to Shreveport for an appointment with Jenny's hairdresser. They confer behind Sally's back for a few minutes; then he goes to work giving her a new hairstyle. Gone are her long locks, replaced with a short, shaggy, much younger-looking style. Next Jenny takes her to a very chic and expensive clothing store. Sally protests she can't afford to shop here, but Jenny waves her off with this being a belated Christmas present. They leave with several outfits that are casual and youthful. Jenny says as they drive back home, "He won't know what hit him. You look fabulous, Sally."

Sally enjoys the remainder of her visit with her parents and Jenny and Michael, but she grows more and more eager to get back to Atlanta and see Bill.

Sally is back at work for a week before Bill returns from Christmas break. He calls her and asks if he can stop by that night. She waits, anxious to see him as time for his arrival approaches. She is dressed in one of the outfits Jenny bought her. Finally the hour arrives, and he knocks on her door. She opens the door...and each stands staring at the other, speechless. Finally, Bill says, "Wow, you look great. I really like the hair."

Sally asks, "What is that under your nose?"

"That, my dear, is a moustache. I think it makes me look much more distinguished."

They hug and kiss; then they have an enjoyable supper together. After Jody has been played with, read to, prepped for bed, and tucked in for the night, they sit on the sofa and talk. "I really missed you, Bill," Sally confides. "I couldn't wait to see you again."

"Same here, Red. I thought of you all the time. I made a decision. I'm ready to move on to the next level with our relationship."

"Next level? You mean sex?"

"Making love together, not just sex. I know I want you and, if I'm not mistaken, when we kiss I sense you want me as well. I want us to become more committed to each other."

"I'd be lying if I said I didn't want to make love with you. But we can't do it with Jody asleep in the room next door. I'd be too uncomfortable, and what if he came in and caught us? And we can't go to your apartment after he's in bed; I won't leave him alone. There's just no good time to have sex while raising a five-year-old child."

"Well, I'd at least like for us to have a special dinner alone this Saturday night to celebrate being back together. Can you arrange a sitter for Jody? I'll make reservations at the restaurant of your choice, just as long as they don't serve their meals quickly on plastic or paper plates."

The arrangements are made. On Saturday the sitter arrives shortly before Bill comes to pick up Sally. As they head toward the parking lot and Bill's battered Civic, Bill says, "I need to run by my apartment to get my umbrella. It is supposed to storm tonight. I'll only be a minute."

"I'll go with you." As they reach the apartment, Sally sees the lights are out. "Where are your roommates?"

"They're both out of town this weekend." He finds his umbrella. "Got it! We'd better get going; our reservations are for eight o'clock, and they won't hold them if we're late."

Sally pushes him back inside and closes the door behind her. "What *are* you thinking?" She kisses him passionately and feels him respond.

"What about our reservations?"

"Quit talking and take me to the bedroom." Bill picks her up and, kissing her, carries her to his bed. The next four hours are spent in passionate lovemaking like Sally has never experienced before. Finally, they stop. Sally says, "Wow! That was amazing. I learned at least six new positions. I didn't think you were ever going to get tired and stop. I'm going to call you 'Stud' for the rest of my life."

"I didn't get tired. I could never tire of making love with you. I ran out of condoms. I would have stocked up if I'd known we were going to make love tonight. I only had ten on hand. My father always told me that every man should be so fortunate as to experience the love of a redheaded woman at least once in his life. Now I know what he meant. You are *fantastic!*"

This night begins a new chapter in their relationship. Somehow in the coming weeks they find a way to have a lovemaking session at least once a week.

Chapter Six

The next three months fly past. It is now the first week of April. Bill's graduation at the end of May is rapidly approaching, and he has several offers for good jobs to consider. One evening as Sally is preparing supper, she overhears Bill in the living room reading a book to Jody. "Once upon a time, there was this lovely lady who had red hair..."

"Like Mommy," Jody interrupts.

"Just like your mommy. And she had a five-year-old son named Jody..."

"Just like me," Jody interrupts again.

"Yes, exactly like you. Into their life rode a shining young knight on a white horse. The knight fell madly in love with the red-haired lady and with her son, too. The knight wanted to marry the lady and help her raise the boy."

"This book doesn't say that. You're not reading the book," Jody declares.

"No. This is a true-life story. What if I told you the red-haired lady was your mommy and you were the boy. That would make me the knight. Do you think the knight...I...should ask your mommy to marry me? Would you like to have me as a step-father?"

"Would you be around all the time then?"

"Yes, I would. We would all live together. Would you like that?"

"That would be nice. Now read the book the right way," Jody commands.

Sally is standing in the doorway crying. "I also think it would be nice," she says.

Bill walks over to her, takes her in his arms, kisses her, then drops to one knee. "Sally Jeffers, will you do me the honor of marrying me?" He smiles up at her, his eyes glistening with tears. He takes a small jewelry box out of his pocket and hands it to her. Inside is a diamond engagement ring. "The diamond is small, but my love for you is huge," Bill says, choked with emotion.

"Yes. Oh, yes, yes, yes." They hug and kiss, until Jody hollers out, "What about reading my book?"

That night Sally calls Jenny with the news. Jenny is thrilled to hear Sally so joyful. They begin making plans for a June wedding.

The next day Bill informs Sally that he broke the news by telephone to his parents after he returned to his apartment last night and that his mother is flying down from Boston to meet Sally. He asks if she could arrange to take a long lunch on Wednesday so that the three of them could meet. Sally agrees. "How did they take the news of our engagement?" Sally asks.

"Fine. They were happy for me. Mother said she couldn't wait to meet you."

On Wednesday Sally arrives early for their lunch appointment. She paces back and forth in front of the restaurant, unable to stand still as she waits. Five minutes later, Bill arrives with his mother. Mrs. Morris is an imposing woman, tall and slender, with red hair mixed with gray. *"Why, Bill's mother is a redhead,"* Sally thinks, somewhat surprised that he had never mentioned it. She is dressed impeccably, with an obviously expensive designer dress. Introductions are made, and they enter the restaurant together to be seated for lunch. They make small talk as they study the menu; then they place their orders. Mrs. Morris asks Sally, "How old did you say you are, my dear?"

Sally hesitates, her eyes revealing that her mind is racing to come up with a number. "Twenty-seven."

Mrs. Morris continues, "And Bill tells me that you have had two previous husbands. Might I inquire what made those marriages fail?"

"I married as a teenager just to escape where I was living. He was my ticket to Dallas. We were too young and not enough in love. We went our separate ways in a matter of months. My second marriage lasted for five years. We were happy and had a son, Jody, who is now five. We divorced because my husband's pregnant mistress came to me to inform me of their long-time affair and of his promise to divorce me and marry her. I filed for divorce immediately thereafter."

"Bill has told us precious little about your background. Where did you attend college?"

"I never went to college. I went to business school to become a secretary. I have done well at my career. I was recently promoted to personal secretary to a vice-president of a national insurance company."

"Doing well is relative, dear. You are still just a secretary. Did Bill tell you that he has a fellowship offer to attend M.I.T. and do graduate study?"

"Why, no. He told me he has several good job offers..."

"Mother, that is quite *enough*. You have no right to interrogate Sally like this. Stop it, or Sally and I will leave you sitting here," Bill interjects.

Mrs. Morris seems upset by her son's strongly worded outburst. "I must go to the powder room to freshen my makeup. Sally, please accompany me, dear."

Bill says, "Sally, you can stay here with me."

"No, it'll be fine. I don't mind going with her."

As soon as they are inside the Ladies' Room, Mrs. Morris turns to Sally and says, "Just how old are you,

Sally? I could tell you were lying about being twenty-seven."

"I am really twenty-nine. That's still only six years older than Bill."

"Bill is twenty-one. You are *eight* years older. You're a mother. Put yourself in my place. Bill is young, with a chance to spend the next five or six years carefree and improving his future. Wouldn't you want *your* son to go to M.I.T. to further his education, rather than dropping out of school now to take a job with a limited future? Would you want your son to marry an older woman who has been married twice before? Would you want him to give up being single to raise another man's child? My dear, you may have thought you trapped yourself a free ride for you and your son, but there will be no wedding as long as I draw breath. You'll have to go catch someone else's son."

Mrs. Morris' tirade stuns Sally and causes her to burst into tears. "It's not like that. We love each other. I didn't pursue Bill. He chased after me. You're wrong. Bill loves me."

Another woman enters the room, and, seeing Sally so upset, she starts to ask if she needs help. However, Mrs. Morris quickly gives the woman a look that sends her scurrying out of the room without interfering.

"Well, he'll get over it. Young men his age are notorious for letting the small head do the thinking for the big head. In a year he'll have forgotten all about this nonsense."

"You're wrong. We love each other…"

"I am going back to the table now, and I'm going to tell Bill that you felt ill and had to leave. Then I'm taking Bill back to his apartment to straighten him out. You should stay here long enough to compose yourself, then leave quietly and spare yourself more public embarrassment." With that, Mrs. Morris checks her image in the mirror, smiles, and leaves. It's thirty minutes before Sally can stop sobbing enough to leave the room.

Sally calls Jenny the instant she reaches her apartment, but Jenny can't understand much of what she's saying through her sobs. There is a knock on Sally's door. She hangs up on Jenny and answers the door. There stands a furious Bill.

"The old bitch! I threw her out of my apartment. How dare she treat you that way! Sally, I'm so sorry. Can you ever forgive me for letting her talk to you that way? And can you believe she actually offered to buy me a BMW Roadster if I agreed to break off our engagement and attend M.I.T.? She called you a gold-digger. She thinks you pursued me, instead of my having to woo you. I told her she was dead wrong about you and that we're going to marry in spite of her poison."

"Bill, listen to me. She appealed to me as a mother wanting what was best for her son, just like I'll want what's best for Jody all of his life. She has her facts wrong about my being the one initially to start this and about how deeply I love you. But she *is* right about this not being best for you. You have a chance to go to M.I.T. on a fellowship for graduate training. Even I know M.I.T. is one of the world's best engineering schools, and it's hard to get accepted into grad school there. I can't let you throw that away to marry me and take a routine job. And you're only twenty-one. I'm really twenty-nine. Seems we both lied about our true age. Eight years is a huge difference in one's twenties. I've lived my twenties. You still have yours to live. You need to be free to be young and carefree. Marrying me and having Jody to raise would steal your youth from you. One day in a few years, you'd come to resent all you had to give up...and you'd resent Jody and me. Your mother may be a bitch, but she loves her son...and she's right about us getting married being a mistake for you. Here's your ring back. I just can't do this."

"No, Sally. I love you. You love me. It'll be fine. Don't let what Mother said make you throw away our life together."

"I've made up my mind. I love you. So, I'm letting you have a better life without me than you could have with me. Goodbye, Bill." Sally closes the door and leans her head against it crying. Her tears fall on the door and streak toward the floor.

Through the door, she hears, "Red, don't do this. I love you." Eventually, she hears Bill's footsteps as he walks away.

Chapter Seven

Shortly after Bill walks away from her door, the telephone rings. It's Jenny wanting to know if Sally is all right. Strangely, Sally becomes calm and explains in great detail all that has happened, ending with her having just returned Bill's engagement ring, breaking their engagement. Jenny says, "Oh, Sally, are you absolutely certain that you're doing the right thing? You sounded like you were so happy with Bill. I thought you two were truly in love."

"I do love him...enough not to mess up his life. You were right from the start, Jen. There's too much of an age gap to be spanned. I just got lost in a fairy tale for a while, but I'm thinking straight for the first time in months. It's got to be over. There's no changing my mind about this. Trust me."

Bill makes a concerted effort to change Sally's decision. He tries to talk to her in person every day for a week by knocking on her door, but she waits inside crying softly and refusing to open the door. Sally recognizes his telephone calls with Caller ID, and she refuses to answer. He calls her at work twice, but she hangs up as soon as she recognizes his voice. He sends her a dozen roses for four days in a row, but she leaves them lined up outside her door. Finally, he gives up. Sally sees him across the way twice in her comings and goings from her apartment during the next six weeks. Then, the last of May, she sees him pulling out of the apartment parking lot, heading north to Boston and M.I.T. His new BMW Roadster is piled high with his belongings.

During the weeks between her breaking off the engagement and the end of May, Sally pours herself into her job. Working hard is a salve to her bruised emotions. It distracts her from thinking about Bill, and doing an excellent job with her projects and duties wins her praise that mends her ego. She may be "just a secretary" as Mrs. Morris had expressed it, but she is the best damned secretary in the company. Her extra dedication brings her closer to Sam Burke, who benefits from her efforts by finishing projects on-time or ahead of scheduled due dates so that he appears to be a highly efficient executive. Sally even suggests improvements in some projects, many of which Mr. Burke accepts, again adding to his own reputation. Mr. Burke jokes that some days he feels like he should be working for *her*. "Sally, I don't know how I'd have managed without you in this new vice-president position. Bringing you to Atlanta with me was the best decision I could have made to ensure I succeeded in this promotion," Mr. Burke tells her one day, "I'm giving you a ten percent pay raise. Keep up the hard work, and maybe I'll be president of this company in a few more years."

In July, Sally completes a major project that required her to perform extensive research into company records and to compile tables and charts of numerous facts for Mr. Burke's use. Mr. Burke returns to his office after his presentation of the project at a board meeting; he is smiling broadly. "Sally, you did it again. The project report won me nothing but praise from the board. Grab your purse, and let's go. I am taking you to lunch as a victory celebration."

Sally is thrilled at the news of the favorable reception the report received. This is the first time in her three years of working as his secretary back in Dallas and now here in Atlanta that Mr. Burke has invited her to accompany him to lunch. She glows from the praise he has lavished upon her. He takes her to eat at an upscale restaurant in one of Atlanta's most lavish downtown hotels. "Order anything you like, anything at all. It's charged to the company. Would you like some champagne?"

Sally answers, "Normally I wouldn't drink alcohol and then return to work, but today is a celebration and I'm with the boss, so champagne would be nice. I really appreciate your bringing me to lunch with you, Mr. Burke."

"Call me Sam when we're away from the office. And I should take you to lunch more often. We're a team and have gotten close to each other. I hope you enjoy working for me as much as I enjoy having you as my secretary."

"Oh, I do enjoy working for you, Mr. Burke…"

"*Sam.*"

"All right, if you insist, Sam, and I want you to know how much I appreciate all that you've done for my career in bringing me to Atlanta with you."

Sam smiles at her and says, "So, you're happy with your job? I suppose the increased salary and recent pay raise have allowed you to have a higher standard of living as well?"

Sally gushes, "I absolutely love my job. And I don't know how to thank you enough for the generous salary you're paying me, although I do feel that I earn it."

The waiter brings the soup course, and they turn their attention to their meals. After the soup comes the salad, followed by their entrees. Mr. Burke is served the largest steak Sally has ever seen. She has a lobster, crab, and cheese casserole. Mr. Burke insists they try the bread pudding for dessert. During lunch, Sally has one glass of champagne. Mr. Burke has four. After the dessert dishes have been cleared away, Sally says, "Look how late it's gotten. We'd better get back to work before someone complains about my being away so long. I want to thank you again for this lunch, Mr. Burke…"

"Sam, dammit. Call me Sam. And nobody will care how long you are away from your desk. They know you're with me."

"Still, I would feel better about not being gone too much longer."

"You know how at the start of the meal you said how much you wanted to thank me for your promotion and the very generous salary I pay you but didn't know how to thank me? Well, I'll tell you how you can thank me. We're not going back to work today. I have a room upstairs waiting for us. You can show me how appreciative you are up there." Mr. Burke smiles lasciviously, as he reaches across and takes her hand in his.

Sally recoils in horror. She pulls her hand away from his grasp and stammers, "That will never happen, *Mr. Burke.* I'm willing to say that you are making a mistake because you drank far too much champagne. Otherwise, I could file a sexual harassment complaint against you."

"Go ahead and file your complaint. It's your word against mine, and I'm a company vice-president and you're just a secretary. Who do think will win that one? Now, you'll either accompany me upstairs, or you'll be reassigned to the secretarial pool and we'll see how you like living on *that* salary. The choice is yours!"

"If you demote me, I'll take you to the board of directors. I am leaving now and returning to work." Sally gets up and storms out of the restaurant. She returns to her desk, waiting nervously to see what will happen when Mr. Burke returns. However, he doesn't come back to work that afternoon.

Sally calls Jenny as soon as she and Jody get home that evening. She picked up fast food for Jody's supper, and she gets him started with his meal as the phone is ringing. "Jenny, you're not going to believe what happened today at work! I may be in danger of losing my job." She goes on to describe the events at lunch with Mr. Burke and his threats against her.

"You need to get a lawyer involved right now before he fires you." Jenny chuckles and continues, "You're in luck there. We just happen to have a whole family full of Atlanta lawyers. Let me make a few calls, and I'll get back to you."

Fifteen minutes later, the phone rings. "This is Ken Garrott. You may remember me from Mike and Jenny's wedding."

Sally replies, "Of course, I remember you, Ken. How could I ever forget Agent Brown, or was it Agent Jones?"

"You know about that, do you?"

"Of course, Jenny and I tell each other everything. We're like sisters."

"Jenny just called me to ask me for advice for you in your current job difficulty. Could you meet me for breakfast before work to discuss your options?"

"That would be great. I appreciate the help. Just tell me where and what time."

They make arrangements to meet the next morning. Shortly after they hang up, the telephone rings again. This time it's Jenny. "Hi, Sally. I talked to Michael's brother Ken and to his father. Someone should call you soon."

"Ken just called. We're to meet before I go to work in the morning. Thanks for the help, Jen. I feel much better knowing I have a lawyer to talk to about this."

Sally has a restless night, barely getting any sleep. She can never get her mind to slow down enough to fall soundly asleep. She takes Jody to school early so he can have breakfast there; then she goes to meet Ken.

Ken is waiting outside for her. She walks up to him and says, "Hi, Ken, I'm Sally. Thanks for meeting me." From the blank look on his face, she's not sure he recognizes her.

"My God, Sally. You have sure changed from when I last saw you. I wouldn't have recognized you."

Sally smiles at his comment.

Over breakfast, they discuss Sally's predicament at work and what her options are. Ken advises, "Your boss definitely has the upper hand here. The other executives are going to believe what he tells them over whatever you say, unless you have proof. You need witnesses or some evidence in writing, like a note or email from him. Are there any other secretaries that he's sexually harassed that will testify on your behalf – that sort of thing. If he fires or demotes you, you need to go immediately to your Human Resources Office and file a sexual harassment complaint. Then go to the president of the company's office and ask for an appointment to see him immediately to report your boss's actions. He will probably refuse to see you, but we want it on record that you tried to inform him. Should you get fired or even demoted, we can file a lawsuit against your boss *and* against the company. Unfortunately, if we end up in court without any evidence incriminating him, it's your word against his again, and the company will fight dirty. They'll parade a long line of company employees and executives in to testify to his impeccable character and to your poor job performance and emotional instability due to your recent broken engagement."

"You know about my breaking my engagement?"

"Jenny told me last night when she was giving me some background for the case. Sorry about your problems with Bill. But, to continue, the best thing you can hope for is that Mr. Burke will come in to work today and act as though nothing ever happened. Perhaps he was testing the waters with you, and doesn't plan to pursue his threats any further. Maybe it was the champagne talking. You can only hope. Any questions?"

"No, I think you've covered all the options. Except, how much would it cost if I have to file a lawsuit and we actually end up going to court?"

"Jenny said to tell you that you're family. There'll be no charge. Okay, that about covers things. I need to get to court. Please call me if there are any further developments that require my services. Good morning to you." Ken hurries off to court, and Sally nervously goes to work.

Mr. Burke arrives at his usual time. He smiles at Sally and gives her his usual, cheerful "Good morning, Sally. How are you today?" as he walks past her desk. Shortly thereafter he emerges from his office and informs her that he'll be in the president's office should anyone need him. Again he acts as pleasant as he normally is. Sally thinks that yesterday's unpleasantness appears to have been forgotten. She breathes a sigh of relief.

Her sense of being out of trouble soon evaporates. Betty Roberts, the president's secretary and Sally's close friend, calls her. "What's going on with you and Mr. Burke? He's in with my boss now, and I overheard him saying that lately you've become erratic in your work and emotionally unstable. He plans to move you to the secretarial pool later today. What's up, Sally? Why's he doing this to you?"

161

"Damn! The bastard! He took me to lunch yesterday and propositioned me. He threatened me that if I didn't go upstairs at the hotel right then and have sex with him that he would fire me from this job. Dammit!"

"Well, he finally got around to *you*, eh? He's worked his way through half the secretarial pool since he got here, either by wooing them with fancy meals and bonuses or by threatening them with loss of their job. You work for a real asshole, Sally."

"Why haven't you ever mentioned this to me before?"

"I figured you knew. Also, I didn't know if you were one of his conquests."

"Could you give me a list of all the secretaries he's seduced? It would be mighty helpful to have."

"I could make a list for you, but it would be guesswork. I don't think many, or maybe any, would admit to it."

"I'd appreciate a list anyway."

In half an hour Mr. Burke returns and stops by her desk. "You have an appointment with Human Resources at ten o'clock." He turns and enters his office. Sally follows him inside and closes the door.

"Mr. Burke...Sam, I've been thinking about yesterday. I may have acted too hastily. It's just that you caught me off guard. My ex-husband cheated on me; that's why I divorced him. The idea of me cheating with you behind your wife's back just didn't sit well with me at first, but now that I've had more time, I *do* feel the need to repay you for being so kind to me. I want to show you my appreciation, and this would be the perfect way for me to thank you for all the generosity that you've shown toward me. Will you give me another chance?" Sally smiles her sweetest smile.

Complete shock registers on Mr. Burke's face; then it's replaced with a look of delight. "Glad to see you be so sensible. We'll have lunch today then."

"You already have a lunch appointment with a Mr. Pell and a Mr. Langworth. Should I call them and cancel? When would you like me to reschedule with them?" Sally's heart is racing, as she tries to appear perfectly calm.

"Damn! No, I need to keep that appointment. We'll have our lunch tomorrow. Clear my schedule for the afternoon tomorrow."

"Whatever you say, Sam."

Chapter Eight

The telephone is ringing as Sally opens the door to her apartment that evening; it's Jenny, anxious for an update. "Hi, Sally, tell me what happened with your meeting with Ken and then what happened at work today."

Sally tells all about her discussion with Ken and the new developments at work.

"You don't plan to actually have sex with the bastard, do you?" Jenny asks, anger filling her voice.

"I was just buying some time. Otherwise, I'd have been demoted from my job today. I needed time to think over my options. Maybe I could get some of the women on Betty's list to come forward. I'll think of something. Maybe I'll give Ken a call later."

Jenny says, "That might be wise. He must be working on your case already. After your talk this morning, he called me and asked all about you. He had dozens of questions about you. He knows your history clear back to when we met in high school."

"Why would he need to know all that? That has nothing to do with this case."

"He said it would help him know how to proceed. He's a good lawyer. He's always quite thorough and extremely well-prepared when he goes to court."

Sally spends another restless night. In the morning she goes to work as usual. Mr. Burke grins at her when he arrives at work. As he passes her desk, he asks, "Are we still on for lunch today?"

Sally smiles coyly. "Why, of course, Sam. Why wouldn't we be?"

The remainder of the morning, Mr. Burke grins at her like a wolf about to slaughter a young lamb. Sally smiles back, although her skin feels like it's crawling. Lunchtime arrives, and Mr. Burke says, "Let's go. I can hardly stand the wait." They drive in his car to the same hotel; however, this time he intends to go straight up to a room. "We can order room service afterwards...or in between rather," he smirks as they enter the lobby.

Sally replies, "How about a drink in the bar first? It'll relax me and make me more in the mood."

"Sure, one quick drink won't hurt, I guess."

They enter the bar and perch themselves on bar stools. Sally lays her purse on the bar as she adjusts herself on the stool. They order their drinks; then Sally says, "You're the most important man I'll ever have had sex with...a company vice-president." Mr. Burke grins at the flattery. Sally continues, "Too bad it has to be under threat of losing my job if I refuse."

"You'll enjoy it anyway, honey. I'm quite good in the sack, if I do say so myself. Women purr like kittens when I get through with them," he says smugly.

"Just to clear the air, Mr. Burke, uh, Sam, is this a one-time deal? If I have sex with you today, I'll get to keep my job forever, or will you expect more?"

"Well, you get a large paycheck every two weeks. I think you should plan on thanking me every two weeks to ensure those paychecks keep coming."

"You expect me to have sex with you every two weeks if I want to keep from losing my job?"

"That sounds fair enough to me. Finish your drink. I'm tired of just *talking* about sex, and I'm ready to get to it." He stands up and, taking hold of her arm at the elbow, leads her toward the elevator. They ride up to the eleventh floor and search for room 1146. He opens the door and guides her inside. He then takes hold of her and kisses her hard on the mouth as his hands begin probing her body.

Sally pushes him away and says, "Slow down. I need to use the bathroom. Why don't you get undressed and get in bed? I'll only be a minute." She carries her purse into the bathroom with her. She waits for a minute to pass. She continues to wait until Mr. Burke calls out, "Come on out. I am getting tired of waiting for you."

Sally walks out of the bathroom. Mr. Burke is lying naked on the bed. At the sight of her still fully clothed, he stands up and says, "What are trying to pull? Why do you still have on your clothes?" Sally pulls a camera from behind her back and clicks away. Mr. Burke instantly becomes enraged and storms toward her. His feet became entangled in his clothes piled on the floor beside the bed. Sally shoves him backwards onto the bed, scoops up his clothes, and runs out into the hallway. She then calmly walks to the elevator, rides down to the lobby, and walks over to a waiting Mrs. Burke. "So nice of you to meet me here, Mrs. Burke," Sally says. "We won't be doing lunch after all. Your husband is up in room 1146. He's buck naked and ready for sex. I decided that I didn't want to have sex with him. Perhaps *you* do." She hands the pile of clothes to a bewildered Mrs. Burke and leaves.

Chapter Nine

At precisely ten o'clock the next morning, Sally and Ken approach Betty Roberts' desk, and Ken announces, "We have an appointment to see Mr. Thompsun. My office called earlier this morning."

Betty says, "Of course. He's expecting you." As they pass her desk, she gives Sally a quizzical look, and Sally winks at her and smiles wryly.

They walk into the president's office; he stands up behind the desk and extends his hand. They exchange handshakes and introductions. Mr. Thompsun says, "I've asked the head of our legal department to join us. I assume you have no objections."

"Not at all. His being here will speed things along," Ken answers. Mr. Thompsun presses a button on his speaker and tells Betty to send in the lawyer, who promptly joins the gathering.

Ken speaks, "Let's get right to it, shall we? My client Mrs. Sally Jeffers here has been sexually harassed by one of this company's executives, a Mr. Sam Burke. This has caused her a tremendous amount of emotional and psychological pain and suffering. She has had to worry about the loss of her job -- a job for which she sold her house in Texas, uprooted her established life there, and left behind all her friends and her son's friends and family to move herself and her young son across the country to serve the needs of this company. She was blackmailed to have sex or lose her job, the prototypical example of sexual harassment at its worst in any company."

The company's lawyer asks, "Is there any proof of these accusations against Mr. Burke, or is this simply a case of a misunderstanding between a vice-president and his secretary -- a woman who has a recent history of severe emotional trauma? If this is his word against hers, then..."

Ken interrupts, "Before we proceed any further, perhaps you should listen to this." He takes from his briefcase the tape recorder Sally had concealed in her purse yesterday and plays a recording of the exchange between her and Mr. Burke at the bar. "Then there are also these." He places a number of pictures of Mr. Burke naked in the hotel room on the desk before the president and the lawyer. "You may keep these, as well as the recording. We have the originals safeguarded," Ken says calmly.

The president shakes his head and asks, "What sort of redress is your client seeking?"

"For her tremendous pain and suffering at being treated so despicably by an officer of this company, we think $600,000 and a letter of recommendation in her behalf signed by you as company president would be in order."

"Considering this is an isolated case and not reflective of company standards, that is totally out of line," the company lawyer interjects. "Mrs. Jeffers may have been embarrassed, but she hardly suffered any significant injury."

"We disagree completely. Mrs. Jeffers suffers from a loss of personal self-esteem, which could impact her ability to ever hold a similar high-paying position again; plus, she has deep emotional trauma from being forced to act in a way abhorrent to her nature. Furthermore, hers is not an isolated incident with this company. Mr. Burke alone has harassed a number of women in positions inferior to his within this company. Here is a partial listing of such women our investigations have discovered thus far." Ken hands them a copy, clearly marked PRELIMINARY FINDINGS, of the list Betty provided to Sally. "And this does *not* include cases of sexual harassment within this company by *other* executives." At this statement, Mr. Thompsun's eyebrows arch, then return to normal position. Ken concludes, "I feel certain that upon careful consideration of how this case will play in the headlines, you'll decide that Mrs. Jeffers' settlement offer is quite reasonable."

"You have a weak case, counselor, and we will let you take us to court. I think you should..." the company lawyer is saying until he's quickly interrupted by Mr. Thompsun. "I think Mrs. Jeffers's settlement offer is eminently fair. Mr. Garrott, if you'll leave the settlement proposal with me, I'll see that it is executed and filed this afternoon. My lawyers will be in touch. I assume that will be satisfactory?"

"Quite satisfactory," Ken answers. He and Sally stand and exit the room. Sally starts to say something, but Ken shakes his head 'no' and whispers "Keep quiet." They ride the elevator down in silence and exit into the parking garage. Once they're seated in the car, Ken breaks into a huge grin. "Well, that went rather well!"

Sally stamps her feet and sways side to side in her sitting position inside the car, causing the car to rock in the process. "Holy shit! $600,000. Holy shit! You were amazing. You blew them away. Holy shit!" Then she laughs and laughs. As they drive back to the Garrott law offices, Sally takes out her cell phone and calls Jenny. "Girl, you are *not* going to believe what just happened!"

Chapter Ten

With the settlement money now in hand, Sally decides to take some time away from working in order to attend college. She thinks she might make a good lawyer one day. She knows she's smart enough to have been the company's best secretary, who could have single-handedly taken on many of the projects requiring research, reading and analyzing data, facts, and figures. She is confident that she has what it takes to succeed first in college, then in law school. When she tells Jenny of her plans, Jenny asks, "Are you certain that's what you want at this point in your life? You're talking about being in school until you're thirty-six."

Sally answers, "Hey, I just did things backwards. I worked first; now I'll attend college. It's what I truly want to do. Trust me."

"What about ever getting married again? How does that fit in your plans?"

Sally laughs, "I've been married twice and engaged once more. That's enough for one lifetime. I've sworn off men forever."

In September, Sally enrolls in Georgia State University in Atlanta. She's soon loaded down with homework. School and Jody occupy all of her time for months. Her calls to Jenny become less frequent, now reduced to once a month, sometimes less.

Six months pass. During one call to Jenny, Jenny asks, "Still no man in your life?"

Sally replies, "Well, there is someone I see occasionally, but I don't want to say anything more. I might jinx it."

Jenny and Michael get pregnant again; Sally is excited for them. Meanwhile, her studies are going quite well. She's an A student and extremely proud of her academic achievements.

Summer arrives; Sally has completed her freshman year as an honors student, and her confidence has grown considerably. She's now a self-assured thirty-one-year-old woman with a bright future ahead of her. However, Jody has grown unhappy with living in Atlanta. Nearly seven years old and in second grade, he doesn't like his school, and he dislikes having to spend so much time in after-school programs due to his mother's busy schedule. With the hours Sally is spending in classes and studying, Jody feels neglected. Sally feels guilty and even briefly considers letting her ex-husband have custody of Jody, thinking he might be better off living in Dallas with his father, stepmother, and half-sister. Here in Atlanta, Jody has only his mother. Sally decides she and Jody need a break from their routine this summer. She plans to stay with her parents on White Lightning Road for two months.

Their summer weeks are spent as an extended vacation. Jody gets all the attention he needs from his grandparents. In addition, Michael takes him fishing and exploring the woods regularly. Sally and Jenny rejuvenate their friendship as well. They shop in Shreveport at the new shopping centers along Youree Drive, including the expensive chic stores that Sally once avoided. They have lunches in Ruston and other small communities in the area. Sally becomes acquainted with many of Jenny's friends. Sally sees how happy Jenny is living here, and she even becomes a little envious of Jenny's easy-going rural lifestyle. After seven weeks, Jenny asks, "Why don't you move back here? Jody loves living here. You could continue your studies at Louisiana Tech; it's just a short commute from here. You could live in the house Michael and Cathy remodeled. We don't use it, except as a guesthouse. What's to keep you from moving back here?"

Sally replies, "My life is in Atlanta now. I like Georgia State...and I've been dating someone."

"What's this? You've been holding out on me? You're serious enough about someone to stay in Atlanta for him? Who is he? Is he a student at Georgia State with you?" Jenny asks excitedly.

Sally shakes her head. "I'm not telling you *anything*. It might jinx it. I told you too much about Bill. This one I'm keeping to myself. Anyway, we're not *that* serious yet. I'm not sure what will happen."

Jenny pouts. "This'll be the first secret you ever kept from me. I always tell you *everything*." She pokes out her lower lip and looks hurt. "Are you feeling guilty yet?" She laughs and gives Sally a playful shove. "Tell me!"

"This one remains a secret for now. I'll tell you all about it someday, though, I promise."

At the end of August, Sally and Jody return to their apartment in Atlanta, much to Jody's chagrin. Sally gets immersed in her studies again, and Jody enters second grade.

In late October, Jenny tells Sally that someone has purchased the land adjoining her parents' old property where her and Michael's house now stands. "Looks like we'll be getting new neighbors to the west of us, on the Vienna-side of our property. They're clearing a site to build a house on a hilltop, overlooking the woods behind the house. They'll have a beautiful view from there. Bubba down at the crossroads store is fit to be tied. He hasn't been able to get a word out of the contractor about who the new owner is. I guess we'll all find out soon enough; they should be finished with construction early next year. Our new baby should be making its appearance in December. Seems like all of the Garrotts plan on being here sometime in December, either for the birth or for Christmas. Why don't you and Jody come stay with us at Christmas as well? I'll understand if you can't make it for the birth if you're in the midst of exams then, but you have *no* excuse for missing Christmas with us."

"Wild horses couldn't keep me away from White Lightning Road this Christmas. I really might miss this birth due to my exams in December, but I've already told my mom and dad to expect us for a long stay. Why don't you just work on keeping that baby inside you until Christmas?"

"Babies have a mind of their own about when they want to enter the world. Maybe it'll be two weeks late."

November and the first two weeks of December pass. Jenny is large with child and more and more ready to give birth with each passing day and each new ache and pain, but the baby seems content to stay where it is. Then Sally arrives with Jody for their Christmas break; that night Jenny goes into labor. Sally rushes to the hospital and tells her, "Thanks for waiting for me. I'd have hated to miss another big event in your life." Jenny has another son. Michael gets to name this one; he names him John James Garrott. Michael's parents arrive to see their new grandson and to stay for Christmas. Jenny brings her new son home three days before Christmas. On Christmas Day the Garrott house is filled with relatives and friends, food and drink, and presents galore. Mid-afternoon, when the house has quieted down, a neighbor stops by to drop off one of his wife's homemade fruitcakes. "Say, I saw someone walking around at that new house they're building up on the hill over yonder. He must be the new owner, eh?"

Jenny suggests to Michael, "Let's drive up there and invite him to come for some coffee and cake. It's the neighborly thing to do."

Michael laughs. "You're just dying of curiosity to learn who our new neighbor is. Okay, let's go meet him and see if he'll stop by our house to get acquainted."

As Jenny and Michael head for their car, Sally asks, "Mind if I tag along?"

Michael says, "The more, the merrier. Come on."

The three of them drive up to the construction site. Parked in front of the partially built house is a rental car. They get out, but see no one. "He must be inside somewhere. Let's look around," Jenny says. They enter the house and begin looking around. Suddenly, from behind them, they hear, "Mike! Jenny!" They turn around to see Ken standing there. "Surprise!" Ken says. Jenny and Michael are shocked at seeing Ken. Sally, however, smiles and walks over to him. They embrace and kiss lovingly.

Jenny's forehead wrinkles in utter surprise as she begins to put the pieces together. "What's going on here? Are you two *a couple*?"

Sally responds, with her arm around Ken's waist, "Meet your new neighbors -- the soon-to-be Mr. and Mrs. Ken Garrott. We got engaged in late September, but we decided to save the news for a Christmas family surprise. Ken is going to practice law in Ruston. The arrangements have already been made. I'll go to school at Louisiana Tech in Ruston until the babies start arriving; we plan on having several. I want all my children to grow up on White Lightning Road, near their relatives and in the piney woods of north Louisiana."

Jenny starts crying. There are congratulatory hugs and kisses all around.

Later that day, Sally says to Jenny when they are alone, "As teenagers living here, could you ever have guessed that the two of us would end up *choosing* to live as neighbors on White Lightning Road? Or that we would be married to brothers? Or that we would be millionaires? Have you stopped to think that now we actually *will* be family? We'll be sisters-in-law – Sally and Jenny Garrott! This is all just too perfect to have ever been able to predict when we were teenage friends."

Jenny responds, "Sometimes you have what you need in life right before you and you just can't see it. But we both managed to find it. I'm so happy that we're going to be friends, neighbors, and sisters all our lives and that we'll get to watch our children grow up together. We'd never be as happy living anywhere else than right here on White Lightning Road. Trust me."

Other Books By This Author

Poetry For The Common Man: Storoems and Poems
2003
ISBN 1411600649

Gilleland Poetry: Storoems and Poems
2005
ISBN 1411629272

Bob the Dragon Slayer
2005
ISBN 1411633156

www.ingramcontent.com/pod-product-compliance
Lightning Source LLC
Chambersburg PA
CBHW020438180626
46812CB00003B/1298